Maurice Procter and ⠇⠅⠑ Murder Room

>>> This title is part of The Murder Room, our series dedicated to making available out-of-print or hard-to-find titles by classic crime writers.

Crime fiction has always held up a mirror to society. The Victorians were fascinated by sensational murder and the emerging science of detection; now we are obsessed with the forensic detail of violent death. And no other genre has so captivated and enthralled readers.

Vast troves of classic crime writing have for a long time been unavailable to all but the most dedicated frequenters of second-hand bookshops. The advent of digital publishing means that we are now able to bring you the backlists of a huge range of titles by classic and contemporary crime writers, some of which have been out of print for decades.

From the genteel amateur private eyes of the Golden Age and the femmes fatales of pulp fiction, to the morally ambiguous hard-boiled detectives of mid twentieth-century America and their descendants who walk our twenty-first century streets, The Murder Room has it all. >>>

The Murder Room
Where Criminal Minds Meet

themurderroom.com

Maurice Procter 1906–1973

Born in Nelson, Lancashire, Maurice Procter attended the local grammar school and ran away to join the army at the age of fifteen. In 1927 he joined the police in Yorkshire and served in the force for nineteen years before his writing was published and he was able to write full-time. He was credited with an ability to write exciting stories while using his experience to create authentic detail. His procedural novels are set in Granchester, a fictional 1950s Manchester, and he is best known for his series characters, Detective Superintendent Philip Hunter and DCI Harry Martineau. Throughout his career, Procter's novels increased in popularity in both the UK and the US, and in 1960 *Hell is a City* was made into a film starring Stanley Baker and Billie Whitelaw. Procter was married to Winifred, and they had one child, Noel.

Philip Hunter

The Chief Inspector's Statement (1951)
   aka *The Pennycross Murders*
I Will Speak Daggers (1956)
   aka *The Ripper*

Chief Inspector Martineau

Hell is a City (1954)
   aka *Somewhere in This City*
The Midnight Plumber (1957)
Man in Ambush (1958)
Killer at Large (1959)

Devil's Due (1960)

The Devil Was Handsome (1961)

A Body to Spare (1962)

Moonlight Flitting (1963)
   aka *The Graveyard Rolls*

Two Men in Twenty (1964)

Homicide Blonde (1965)
   aka *Death has a Shadow*

His Weight in Gold (1966)

Rogue Running (1966)

Exercise Hoodwink (1967)

Hideaway (1968)

Standalone Novels

Each Man's Destiny (1947)

No Proud Chivalry (1947)

The End of the Street (1949)

Hurry the Darkness (1952)

Rich is the Treasure (1952)
   aka *Diamond Wizard*

The Pub Crawler (1956)

Three at the Angel (1958)

The Spearhead Death (1960)

Devil in Moonlight (1962)

The Dog Man (1969)

Devil in the Moonlight

Maurice Procter

An Orion book

Copyright © Maurice Procter 1962

The right of Maurice Procter to be identified as the author of this work
has been asserted in accordance with the Copyright, Designs and Patents
Act 1988.

This edition published by
The Orion Publishing Group Ltd
Orion House
5 Upper St Martin's Lane
London WC2H 9EA

An Hachette UK company
A CIP catalogue record for this book is available from the British Library

ISBN 978 1 4719 0257 4

www.orionbooks.co.uk

1

DETECTIVE CONSTABLE MAFFIN tapped on the half-open door of Chief Inspector McCool's office and intruded his head. He said: 'A P.C. just brought in Johnny Rodrick, sir. Caught him in Sayle's.'

'So he's the one,' said McCool. He and his staff had been mildly worried about a recent series of evening shop-breakings. He turned away from his desk and rose to his feet. 'We'll hear what he has to say.'

Maffin stood aside from the doorway, his hard, dark, reckless-looking face alive with expectation. 'Now we might clear some stuff, sir,' he said.

McCool nodded. Rodrick's reaction to a clean capture would be typically professional. An unprofitable man to talk to normally, he would make a clearance of every crime he had committed as soon as he realized that a conviction was certain.

Thinking about that, the detective inspector led the way through the main C.I.D. office and along the corridor to the charge-room. Walking behind, Maffin looked up at him. McCool was noticeably tall even among policemen. His long legs were moving in a strolling gait, but to stay at his elbow Maffin had to stride.

'Elegant bastard,' Maffin mused, without rancour. McCool had led him into and out of trouble many a time, and that well-tailored back was as familiar to him as the lean, handsome face. Had it not been for his broad shoulders, the man would actually have been slender, but he was known to have a backbone like a steel spring and a punch like a striking python. In the days when young policemen had been broken in on hard, pugnacious Irish labourers instead of Teddy Boys, the probationer McCool had proved that he knew how to fight. Now, when he was head of the town's Criminal Investigation Department, that tough reputation was still remembered.

He led the way into the charge-room, which was conveniently placed behind the front office, and between that office and the cell corridor. He came upon a scene which was common enough in there. The prisoner, Rodrick, and a young constable in uniform were glowering at each other, while a burly, placid gaoler was going through Rodrick's pockets. The station sergeant was standing by with his pen poised over the charge book.

'Name?' the sergeant was asking.

'Same as last time,' Rodrick snapped.

The sergeant's expression did not change. 'Same name,' he said, as he began to write. 'Same address, same occupation, same useless bloody nuisance.'

'You can talk. Wait till the beak sees this eye.'

McCool had already noticed Rodrick's black eye. 'Somebody hit you?' he asked pleasantly.

Rodrick, a wiry man of medium height, about thirty years old, glared along his rat nose at the constable. 'He did. I'll get him the sack for it.'

The constable, named Berry, was a few years younger and a good deal bigger and heavier. And he was indignant. 'Look here. sir,' he protested. He stooped and pulled up a leg of his blue uniform trousers. Above a glossy black boot and a thick woollen sock a hacked shin could be seen. 'He tried to kick me feet from under me,' the youngster explained. 'I hit him accidentally while I was getting a hold on him.'

2

'That's a tale,' Rodrick fumed. 'The inspector knows I don't fight bobbies. It's the kick was an accident.'

'I hear you found him in Sayle's,' McCool interposed.

'Yessir.' Berry was rather proud of that. 'I found one of the back doors jemmied. I started to go in, and then I thought I'd better comply with General Orders and get the place surrounded. Then the burglar alarm went off, just for a few seconds. I knew then he'd be away in a minute, so I went in. He came running down the main staircase right into me arms.'

'So you arrested him. Was he alone?'

The young man's pride began to evaporate. He became aware of pitfalls. 'I—I think so, sir.'

'Did you bring him out the back way?'

'No, sir. One of the front doors has a latch. I just waltzed him out that way and slammed the door behind me.'

'Then the back door is still open? Who's looking after the place?'

Berry was completely deflated. 'Nobody, sir. I was just going to mention it.'

McCool's glance slid to Maffin. 'Bring my car round,' he said softly, and Maffin departed in haste.

'Did you look into Sayle's office at all?' McCool went on.

'No, sir,' the P.C. confessed. 'I had me hands full with this fellow.'

'He's made a proper orchestra stalls of it,' Rodrick crowed. 'They'll be sending him home to Mamma.'

'Be careful. He might close your other eye,' McCool warned him, in his deceptively gentle voice. 'Did you have a mate in there?'

'You'd better go and look, Copper.'

A hard glint suddenly appeared in the inspector's eyes, and Rodrick was reminded of something he had temporarily forgotten—that Copper McCool would put up with a little insolence, but only a little. He stepped back a pace although McCool had not moved.

There was one more question, which had to be asked there and then. 'How long have Sayle's had a burglar alarm?' the inspector wanted to know.

The station sergeant replied. 'They haven't, sir.'

'I distinctly heard it,' the P.C. said. 'It was like a little bell, but quite loud. It went for about ten seconds. I thought Rodrick had started it, and then cut the circuit or something.'

McCool turned to Rodrick. 'Did you hear it?'

'He's dreaming,' the prisoner said scornfully. 'I heard no burglar alarm.'

'You couldn't,' said the sergeant. 'There isn't one.'

McCool was turning away. 'I want the place surrounded,' he said. 'And get on to the fire station and see if they know anything about an alarm.'

He went out of the building with long, swift strides. His plain C.I.D. car, a big Humber, was at the kerb, and Maffin was at the wheel. McCool slipped into the seat beside him and the car sped along quiet Bull Row which gave its name to the police buildings, around the big circular rose garden which made the Horsemarket roundabout, down the wide main street called Commonside to Sayle's Store.

The shop windows along this wide, straight thoroughfare were brilliantly lighted, eclipsing the glare of the sodium street lights. Sayle's big display windows were possibly the brightest of all. Selwyn Sayle might quibble at the cost of burglar alarms and fire precautions, but he would spare no expense in drawing attention to his wares.

Maffin stopped the car in front of the stores. No other car stood at the kerb there, and at that time, half past nine, there were only a few people in sight. As McCool alighted he stared around, sniffing the air of the clear, dark

4

October night. His glance moved along the darkened upper windows on both sides of the street. This was pure habit, as was his look at every pedestrian and every car in view.

The two detective officers went along the alley which led to the yard behind Sayle's. In the yard they found a door which had been deeply bitten by a jemmy in a ruthless hand. McCool glanced briefly at the riven jamb, then switched off his flashlight. He and his companion followed the recent example of P.C. Berry, and entered Sayle's in darkness. They were in a stock-room, and they saw a clear way through it to an open doorway where faint light invited them. They passed through to the ground floor of the shop itself, and this, at first, appeared to be a place of strong moonlight. The 'moonlight' came indirectly from the display windows, through the clear space above the rich, heavy curtains which screened the interior of the shop from window-gazers.

McCool stared around. The long counters shone darkly. Glass and bright metal glimmered. He imagined that he could smell metal, because this department sold every kind of hand tool on the market. And each tool was the best obtainable, and priced accordingly.

The silence, the stillness and the eerie glow had no effect on Maffin. He spoke into McCool's ear because that person was behaving as if stealth were necessary. 'Seen the titfer?' he whispered hoarsely.

McCool breathed a reply. He had seen the hat. It was lying on the counter which was nearest to the small front door with the latch lock. To him there was something very strange about that hat, because Johnny Rodrick had never worn it and never would wear it. Johnny went bare-headed, winter and summer.

Feeling oddly disturbed, he went and picked up the hat. It was a man's light-grey velour, an expensive piece of headgear in new condition. If Rodrick had had an

5

accomplice that night the man would not have worn a hat like that. It made a complication in what should have been a straightforward case. It was the second complication.

McCool shrugged, and replaced the hat. He was an imaginative man, but also a policeman of much practical experience. There would probably be a simple explanation of the hat, and the so-called burglar alarm as well. He went to one of the window curtains and drew it a little aside to look into the street. The first thing he saw was a police sergeant in uniform, looking at him through the window. The sergeant recognized him and raised a hand in acknowledgement. McCool made a little circle in the air with his finger and moved head and eyebrows slightly in an interrogative manner. The sergeant nodded solemnly.

McCool let the curtain fall into place. 'The shop is surrounded already,' he said aloud, as he turned away from the window. 'If there *is* anybody hiding in here he won't get out. Let's have some light on the job.'

They found light switches, and then they returned to the hat. They looked at it.

'Happen Johnny's been doing a job at Dunn's,' Maffin suggested. 'Picked himself the best lid in the place, just for the hell of it.'

McCool shook his head. He handled the hat again, and looked at the maker's name. 'No owner's initials,' he commented as he put it down. 'Where is Sayle's private office?'

Maffin pointed. 'I think it's tucked away in a corner over there,' he said. 'I've seen Sayle dashing in and out of there when I've been in the shop.'

They went in that direction and found the office, which was the owner's sanctum, a special little room used for special business, and almost a separate concern from his big office upstairs.

The door was open. McCool stood in the doorway and

switched on the light. He gazed at an open safe, and then he turned his head slightly to observe a heap of stained brown gabardine which lay on the floor. It was an untidy sight, even though the legs and feet which protruded from it were expensively trousered and immaculately shod.

2

MAFFIN peered over McCool's shoulder. 'Blimey,' he said. Then: 'I wouldn't have thought it of Johnny.'

'Nor me,' said the inspector tersely. 'But it looks as if he's our client.' He looked at the new claw hammer which lay beside the body. There was not much blood on it, just a thin reddish film on the shiny striking face. He stooped, and carefully raised the woollen gabardine raincoat which covered the body. 'It's Sayle himself,' he said as he let the coat fall gently back into place. 'We don't really need a doctor yet. I never saw a deader one.'

But General Orders were made to be obeyed. Until a doctor had given confirmation a policeman was not allowed to assume that life was extinct. McCool picked up the telephone. His first call was for an ambulance. But immediately afterwards he called the police surgeon. Then he passed on the news to Police Headquarters and issued orders. Then he informed the Chief Constable himself and received them. The Chief's orders were the ones which McCool had already issued. The Chief, able in administration, had never forgotten how to be a practical policeman.

McCool put down the telephone. 'We have just a little more time before the crowd arrives,' he said. 'I wonder what there was in that safe.'

'I heard a rumour,' said Maffin.

McCool had squatted to look more closely at the carpet.

8

'So did I,' he replied, without raising his glance. 'But did he keep it here?'

The story was that Selwyn Sayle, a forceful and greedy man, was in possession of a large sum of money which was an embarrassment to him. He had acquired the money by making cash deals which he had concealed from the Commissioners of Inland Revenue. He had accumulated such a large amount of cash that when he had spent as much as he dared he was afraid to invest the remainder in any normal way. That was the substance of rumour, which is not always a lying jade.

The safe was not as old as some of the safes which McCool had seen, but neither was it modern. The lock appeared to be undamaged, and there was not even a scratch on the bright brass plate which surrounded the keyhole. Obviously it had been opened with a key, and probably with a key from Sayle's pocket. He inspected the contents without touching anything. He could not see any money or anything which looked as if it contained money. But at the bottom of the safe, at the back of the main lower compartment, there was an ominously empty space.

'Nothing much there, but possibly something missing,' he said.

'If Sayle had a lot of cash you'd think he'd have it in a safe deposit,' was Maffin's opinion.

McCool nodded. He strolled out into the shop to see if there were any arrivals at the door. He looked around. It was a fine business, and Sayle had been a person of some importance in the town. Inheriting a valuable ironmonger's shop from his father, he had prospered and expanded on the same site until he was able to stock everything for the journeyman from boxes of screws to power tools, and everything for the home and garden from coal scuttles, hand forks and geysers to fireplaces, refrigerators, cookers, washers, heaters, sinks, air conditioners and the most ornate bath-and-shower arrangements. Once, years ago when continental holidays were mainly the privilege of the rich, he had displayed a *bidet* installation which had aroused more curiosity, speculative gossip, sniggering amusement and scandalized indignation in the town than his own murder was likely to arouse.

McCool's glance roved in search of the source of the murder weapon. The ground floor was the place where ironmongery had always been sold, in Sayle's day as in his father's, and one entire wall behind a counter was lined with small drawers filled with the small items of the hardware trade. Elsewhere were smaller banks of drawers, and tall showcases filled with tools. The inspector looked now at the counter where the hat lay, and at the showcase directly behind it. There was a stand of new hammers on top of the showcase, and a gap in the neat row where one hammer was missing.

Any normal man could have reached up and taken one of those hammers. Johnny Rodrick could have reached, easily.

McCool's gaze moved from the hammers to the hat. That was no longer a mystery, at any rate.

The slam of a car door took him to the window curtains. He saw that an ambulance had arrived. Then a police car drew up, and three men alighted. They were Detective Constable Vickery, P.C. Berry and Johnny Rodrick. They were there on his instructions, but they had arrived a little earlier than he had expected.

McCool moved quickly to switch off all the lights in the shop. 'Get that light out!' he shouted to Maffin, who was still nosing about in Sayle's office. He saw the indirect light from the office vanish, and then he opened the door.

The ambulance men came forward. 'Hold it just a moment, please,' he said to them. 'Be with you in a minute.'

Then he beckoned to the two policemen and their prisoner. 'Come in,' he said. 'We're all ready for you.'

The three men entered, and stood waiting to learn why they were there. McCool let them wait, so that their eyes would become accustomed to the artificial moonlight. Vickery glanced round curiously. Berry and Rodrick, both of them uneasy, stood looking at McCool.

Vickery saw the hat. He stared curiously at it, but made no comment.

Then McCool said to Berry: 'Well, is it just as it was when you were here before?'

'It seems to be, sir. Exactly the same.'

'What about you, Rodrick?'

'It seems the same to me.'

'Was that hat there, on the counter?'

Berry answered quickly: 'Oh no, the hat wasn't there. I assumed that somebody had just now put his hat there.'

'You're sure the hat wasn't there?'

Berry hesitated. 'I'm fairly sure. I don't think I'd have missed seeing it. But I wouldn't go on oath. You see I was excited, concentrating on this man. All I can say with absolute certainty is that I never noticed the hat.'

Rodrick gave a snort of laughter. 'He don't know what day it is. He's a real bright lad, he is. What is all this about this here hat?'

'Are *you* sure it wasn't here?' McCool wanted to know.

'It weren't here when I came in, I'll tell you that. If it had a-been I'd have been off out of here like a scalded cat.'

'But you went upstairs, didn't you?'

'Yes.'

'What brought you down again in such a hurry?'

'Why should I tell you?'

11

'Take my word for it. It'll be better for you if you do.'

Rodrick peered at McCool's face in the pale light. 'I wouldn't take your word on a tanner bet. But there's no harm in telling you. I came down here because I heard summat.'

'What did you hear?'

'Somebody blundering about. This bogey, I expect.'

'Was it something like a burglar alarm that you heard?'

'No.' Rodrick turned to stare in contempt at the man who had arrested him. 'There were no burglar alarm. He's imagined it.'

'And when you came down, you still didn't notice the hat?'

'No. It couldn't have been there.'

Berry intervened, troubled but determined. 'He can't be sure of that, sir. He came down the stairs straight into my hands, and after that he had no time for looking at hats.'

'All right,' said McCool. 'Put the lights on, Maffin.'

When the lights were on, the inspector said: 'Come along, and I'll show you what we found. And you'd better keep your hands in your pockets.'

When he saw the open safe and the body Berry looked sick. He had rushed away with his little thief, and overlooked murder and safe robbery. 'What a schemozzle,' he muttered in despair.

Rodrick's face had turned a dirty grey. He stuttered with fright. 'What's all this? Is that a dead man? I didn't do it. I never came in here.'

'What did the gaoler eventually find in his pockets?' McCool asked.

'Not a thing,' Berry replied. 'Nothing from this place. If he had anything he dumped it before I laid hands on him.'

'No keys?'

'No keys at all, sir.'

'And what's his tale?'

'He says he came round the back of this place to make water, and he saw a door open and he nosed in without felonious intent.'

'He still had his jemmy, didn't he?'

'Yes. He says he picked it up just inside the door.'

'Very weak. It looks as if he's our boy. Take him back to Headquarters, and mind he doesn't slip you.'

'I never did it!' Rodrick wailed as he was taken away. 'I wouldn't kill anybody!'

As the trio went out, Dr. Fraser, the police surgeon, entered. McCool went with him to look at the body. Fraser looked at the bloody smashed skull without a change of expression. 'He made sure,' he commented. 'Like somebody insane. Or in a frenzy. He must have hit him a dozen times. What's your idea about it?'

'Sayle came into the shop by that small front door. He put his hat and raincoat on the counter, probably not switching on the lights. Then he came to do whatever he intended to do. The murderer went and picked up the raincoat, and a hammer from a stand in the shop, came in here and threw the raincoat over the poor man's head and belted him with the hammer.'

'Then?'

'Then he got his keys and opened the safe, if it wasn't already open. What is missing from the safe we don't know yet.'

Fraser gently lifted the battered head to see the face, then looked at the body which still seemed to be crouching away from punishment. 'How old? About sixty?'

'Just about that age, I should think.'

'A dapper little man. That's a good suit he's wearing. All right, I'll see him later.'

'Time of death?'

'Oh, is there some doubt about that?' The doctor brought out his thermometer. Then he tested for *rigor*, which was of course entirely absent at that time. 'Killed only a short time ago. Less than an hour, probably. Certainly not more than two.'

He departed, to let in Sergeant Cole, police photographer, Sergeant Lever, fingerprint expert, and Detective Constable Russett, plans and rough sketches. McCool removed himself so that these people could get on with their work. Vickery had returned, with Detective Sergeant Broadhead. McCool instructed these two, and Maffin, to search the building and pay particular attention to any articles which might be in places where one would not expect them to be. Then he returned to Headquarters.

The main C.I.D. office was deserted except for one officer on stand-by duty. Only two desk lights were burning, and the corners of the long room were in shadow. That was just how McCool wanted it. He had Rodrick brought in, with P.C. Berry in attendance. In the intimate light of a desk lamp a little group arranged itself. The shop-breaker was perched on a stool at the high main desk, and Berry occupied another stool. The man on stand-by was seated near the second lamp, and he waited pen in hand. McCool stood leaning on the desk within reach of the prisoner.

'Just a preliminary chat, Johnny,' he began.

'All taken down in writing,' Rodrick answered bitterly.

'Of course. You've seen enough to know that this is a serious business. You're not obliged to say anything at all, but anything you do say will be taken down in writing and may be given in evidence.'

'All right, you've made it legal. Now that feller can write any lies he likes.'

'The only lies he writes will be the ones you dream up. I

14

don't expect the whole truth, but I'd like enough of it to work on.'

'If you think I'm going to talk myself into trouble you're wrong. You're not going to mix me up in any murder.'

'You're in it already. Johnny on the spot. Unless your mate did it.'

'I didn't have a mate. I was on my tod.'

'Your mate could have been hiding while this constable arrested you. He could have been in Sayle's office. *If* you didn't do the killing your mate could have done it before or after the arrest.'

'I tell you I didn't have a mate.'

'If you didn't you're my boy for the job. If you did you'll have to tell me sooner or later. This is capital murder. You won't shake hands with the hangman for the sake of somebody else. Not you. You'll cough, all right. Especially when we find out your mate got away with a few thousand pounds while you got nothing.'

For a little while astonishment banished the prisoner's fear. 'A few thousand? Was there that much money on the place?'

'We think Sayle had a big sum of money in that safe which was opened.'

'Well, I never saw it. I never saw Sayle either.'

'If you didn't your mate did.'

'I tell you I had no mate. Why do you keep on about that?'

'I want you to get the idea into your thick head. I've got a major crime to clear and I'm going to clear it. Make no mistake about that. It's between two people, you and your mate. If I don't get him I get you.'

The prisoner looked at McCool with deep distrust. He quite believed that the inspector would charge *somebody* with murder, and that he would charge an innocent man if he could not find a guilty one. Moreover, in Rodrick's opinion, he would not particularly care who was his victim, so long as there was a hanging ultimately. For, besides being remembered as a hard hitter, McCool had another reputation. He was known to criminals in his own and neighbouring towns as the most pitiless bastard in the world. This reputation he had built up intentionally, and he fostered it carefully. Through it, he got results. He had no friends *of any kind* in criminal circles. Therefore he had no informers to bring useful items of news. He had always managed without willing informers, and always would. But there had been many unwilling ones, driven to talk by the fear of what McCool would do to them. He carefully encouraged out-and-out crooks to believe that he was a bigger crook than themselves, in the sense that he was totally without conscience in the matter of a conviction. He never hesitated to lie to a liar, if by doing so he could eventually learn the truth. With a trickster he would be tricky, and with a callous thug he would, without raising his voice or his hand, evoke images of maltreatment to make a man tremble.

Fellow policemen who did not actually know him found it hard to believe that his fearsome reputation had been built up entirely by the use of mirrors, as it were. These doubters did not take criminal mentality into consideration. Crooks are liars. Having been convinced by McCool that he would, if necessary, put them away on false evidence, they would subsequently tell their friends that this indeed was what had happened. And naturally they came to believe the lie themselves. They built McCool's reputation for him.

When police officers doubt one of their colleagues their utterances are likely to come to the ears of some member of the Watch Committee. This had happened when McCool was a detective sergeant. It had led to questions in committee and a full-scale inquiry. The Committee had required evidence, not hearsay. There had been none. No hammerings, no elbow-cracking, no perjury, no framed or doctored evidence. There had not even been any unduly long periods of interrogation, because McCool did not work that way. He had emerged from the inquiry with an enhanced reputation as an honest policeman, in the eyes of honest people. Through the gossip of informers and detectives the underworld of the town heard of the inquiry. News of its result was also circulated, leading to only one conclusion. The horrible bastard had foxed the Watch Committee and got away with it again. From that time he had been regarded as invulnerable.

With these matters in the mind Rodrick made his feeble protest. 'You can't prove I did a murder when I didn't. Where's your evidence?'

'My poor lad, you were there, robbing the place,' McCool replied, with a compassion which made the prisoner's skin crawl. 'Anyway, I'll leave you to think about it. I have urgent tasks.' He looked at his watch and spoke to Berry. 'Take him down and charge him with the shop-breaking. That'll hold him nicely while we get our evidence. I've got to carry the sad news to the widow.'

A new voice demanded: 'Whose widow?' and a man moved into the circle of light.

'Hello, Sergeant. What are you doing here?'

'Just passing by on my way home to bed. I heard there was something stirring.'

'There is. A murder job. Selwyn Sayle in his shop.'

Detective Sergeant Hard Times heard the news without emotion. His plain, tough face was still. His eyes, the colour of the sky on a wet day, were completely devoid of feeling. The eyes shifted briefly to Rodrick and back to McCool. 'He do it?'

'He was found on the premises.'

Hard Times allowed himself a faint smile. 'It's a straight

up-and-down job, then,' he said. 'You won't want me.'

McCool thought about that. Hard Times was off duty, and not due in the C.I.D. until nine o'clock in the morning. But this was murder, with every available C.I.D. man working on it, and he had presented himself. If he had not wanted to be involved he ought to have curbed his curiosity and gone quietly home. Besides, he was a very useful man, on a murder or any other job.

Hard Times was speaking again. 'Unless,' he said, looking at Rodrick with calculated malice, 'you want me to talk to this little tea-leaf about some of the uncleared breaks on my list.'

'No, you can do that to-morrow,' McCool decided. 'I've got to go to see Mrs. Sayle. She might be alone. You can come with me.'

'Certainly, sir,' the sergeant said, and McCool was left without the slightest clue as to whether the man was pleased or annoyed. That was all right. McCool didn't care either way.

Hard Times was not the sergeant's real name, though it was said in the force that his wife called him Hardie. It had happened that some policeman visiting his home town of Huddersfield had learned that his father and grandfather had both been called Harry Hard Times, and the name so suited him that it was immediately given to him also. Hard Times was a man for hard roads, hard lines, hard characters and hard cases. He never showed resentment of the nickname, and it was suspected that he rather welcomed it. His real name was Aubrey Viollett, a name so hilariously unsuitable that when he was compelled to utter it in a court of law he always waited stonily for the tell-tale sudden twitch on the face of judge or magistrate.

Rodrick was taken away by Berry, while McCool looked in the telephone directory for the address of the late Selwyn Sayle.

'Fairlawn, Chestnut Park,' he said as he closed the directory.

'I know the house,' said Hard Times.

'Then you can drive,' said McCool, and they went out to his car.

3

FAIRLAWN was a new house of clean new stone. The name was in gilt letters on the stone gateposts. The short, straight drive divided a carefully tended garden which had been laid out with a complete lack of imagination. The house, with its three-car garage at the side, was similar in construction to fifty older houses in Chestnut Park; the same bay windows, stone porch, blue slate roof. It was a fine house designed by an architect who had not been allowed to use a single original idea, if he had had one to use. McCool could readily understand how Selwyn Sayle might have yearned to live in Chestnut Park. When he had achieved his ambition he had demanded a house similar to the dwellings of the other Chestnut Parkers, but newer and therefore better.

As McCool alighted he saw that there were two cars in the garage, which was wide open and well lighted. There was also a bright porch light which spread illumination over the expanse of tarmac in front of the house. Obviously Sayle's return was expected.

The front door stood upon, but an inner door, of glass, was closed. McCool rang the bell. The door was opened by a blonde woman who was not at all startled by seeing two big, hard-looking men on her doorstep. She stood holding the door, looking at them. They looked at her. They had no doubt about her identity, though she was about thirty years younger than her husband. She was very smart, very handsome, very shapely; beautiful in fact. But her beauty was conditioned by the suggestion of hardness, a quality latent yet discernible, which may sometimes be seen in the faces of handsome business women, handsome courtesans, handsome barmaids, handsome actresses. She was a woman who would put a price on her beauty, though she might not sell it. She was Mrs. Sayle, and she knew her way around, and—it seemed obvious—she had married Sayle for his money.

McCool spoke first. Hat in hand, he said 'Good evening', and introduced himself and his companion. 'Could I see Mrs. Sayle?' he asked.

She said: 'I am Mrs. Sayle. Won't you come in?'

They entered. She closed the door and led the way along the hall. Her walk was essentially feminine, very attractive. Her dress might not have been made in Paris, but it looked as if it had.

McCool stole a glance at Hard Times. The sergeant was admiring the lady. It could not be said that his expression had changed much, but his face showed a slightly different sort of impassiveness.

They went into a large, comfortable room which was no doubt referred to as the lounge. Everything in it was modern and expensive, nothing was offensive to a reasonable taste, and nothing was noteworthy. In the style of the times there was a little bar, to which Mrs. Sayle made her way.

'I hope I haven't been running through some red lights,' she said without turning her head. 'Would you like a drink?'

'Not just now, thank you,' McCool said. 'I'm afraid I have some bad news for you. It's about Mr. Sayle, your husband. Mr. Selwyn Sayle, that is.'

The woman turned. 'Has he had an accident?'

'It's much worse than that. Much worse.'

She waited, staring at him.

'He's dead,' McCool told her.

She uttered no cry, and her colour did not change. She dropped her glance away from McCool's and stood still, looking at the floor. Possibly she was looking inward at her own thoughts. At last she answered. 'It's a great shock. I don't know what to say. What happened?'

She looked as if she could stand it. McCool answered: 'He was murdered. In the shop.'

She raised her eyes to look at his. 'By a burglar?'

'By a thief, at any rate. We think so.'

'Was he shot?'

'He was knocked on the head.'

She asked for more specific information than that. He told her of the murder as he believed it had happened. She shuddered when he mentioned the hammer, but continued to listen carefully.

'Was there any special reason for throwing the raincoat over his head?' she asked. 'Surely recognition wouldn't matter.'

'Perhaps we'd better not go into that just now.'

'Tell me. I can take it. I'll have to hear it sometime.'

'Well, when a man is hit very hard on the head with a hammer, blood flies. It gets all over the place, and on the murderer's hands and clothes. He can never be sure that he's clear of it. Mr. Sayle's raincoat is of very high quality. Wool, but very closely woven. It stopped the blood from flying.'

'He was a very cool and cunning murderer, then,' the woman said shrewdly. 'Have you caught him?'

'There is a man under arrest. We caught him in the shop.'

'Who is he?'

'His name is John Rodrick. A bad character.'

For the first time she showed distress. 'Oh dear. Poor, poor Selwyn.'

22

'He wouldn't feel anything. He wouldn't know a thing about it. Why did he go to the shop?'

'I don't know. He didn't tell me he was going to the shop. He just said he had some business. I didn't ask him what it was.'

'Was it unusual for him to go to the shop in an evening?'

'No. He went quite often.'

'To-night is Monday. Did he often go on a Monday?'

'Quite often, but he had no regular night for going.'

'Did he drive himself into town?'

'Yes. Isn't his car standing outside the shop?'

'No. We don't know where it is. Can you give me the description?'

'It's a black Rover.'

'Saloon?'

'Of course. Selywn doesn't—didn't go in for what he called fancy cars.'

'Do you know the number?'

'I'm afraid I don't. I might be able to find the log book, if you'll excuse me a minute.'

She left the room. The two policemen looked at each other.

'She takes it well,' McCool commented in a low voice.

'Not half,' said Hard Times. 'She might be dancing a jig inside herself. She's a rich woman now.'

'A bit of research is indicated.'

'What for? Rodrick did the job, didn't he?'

'Confidentially—and I mean confidentially—I'm fairly certain he didn't do it.'

Hard Times groaned. 'Here we go again. You and Ellery Queen. You can find more twists in a straight case than anybody I know.'

McCool was not annoyed. He and Hard Times had worked together for a long time. 'All right. Forget I said anything,' he advised. 'I want Rodrick to go on thinking he's our Number One suspect. It's the only way I shall ever crack him.'

'I'll crack the little monkey,' said Hard Times. 'Let me talk to him.'

The inspector had no chance to reply, because Mrs. Sayle was coming back with a motor registration book in her hand. She gave it to him.

Both men copied the particulars they required, and then McCool returned the book. Hard Times asked permission to use the telephone, which was in the hall, and then he went to get the car's description circulated.

'Now, Mrs. Sayle,' McCool began. 'I shall have to ask you certain questions. Would you rather I asked them now or later?'

'Ask them now,' she said. She took a cigarette from a silver box on a table, lit it with a silver table lighter and sat down in an armchair.

'May I?' asked McCool, taking a seat opposite to her. Her legs were very nice indeed, he thought, as he tried to avoid looking at them.

'What is it you want to know?' she asked, and he knew that she was aware of his appreciation. He reflected that she might have just heard of the death of a forgotten cousin for all the heartbreak she showed.

'First, your full name,' he began.

'Cherry Sayle. It's spelt "Chérie", but nobody ever has time to pronounce it right.'

'And your occupation is that of housewife?'

'You make it sound very—er—humble. But I suppose it's right. I have no other work.'

'How long have you been married?'

'A little over two years.'

'And your age?'

'Thirty.'

'You were Mr. Sayle's second wife, I believe?'

'Yes. He's—he was thirty-one years older than me. Than I.'

'Have you been married before?'

'No. Would that have mattered?'

'No. This is your personal history for the record, you understand. I must have all the information I can get. In that respect, for the moment, I'm like a reporter.'

'Oh dear. They'll be coming to see me, won't they?'

'I'm afraid so. You may think they're unduly nosy, but they have their job to do. I'm the same, only more so. For instance, I shall want to know if Mr. Sayle carried heavy life insurance. Also, I shall ask you if you were on good terms with him.'

'Oh, I was. We never had a quarrel.'

'I'll bet you had him eating out of your hand,' said McCool, but he said it to himself. Aloud, he returned to the matter of insurance, and was referred to Sayle's accountant.

'Have you any children?' he asked.

'No,' she replied composedly. 'He said he was too old to start bringing up children.'

'Are there any children by the first wife?'

'No.'

'No other heir than yourself, then?'

'He had some cousins last heard of in Sheffield. He hadn't seen either of them for years.'

'Who is his solicitor?'

She gave him a name. He closed his book over his thumb. 'Have you been out this evening?' he asked.

'Not since half past six. I've been shopping in Leeds. I got back in good time for dinner.'

'Mr. Sayle was here when you got back?'

'Yes. We had dinner together. As we usually do—did.'

'And he went to the shop at what time?'

'I can't be sure to the minute. I didn't look at the clock.

It would be sometime around nine. Mrs. Horrocks, our cook, went home just before half past eight, and Selwyn went about half an hour after.'

'Have you any staff living in?'

'No. I have two cleaning women who come in the mornings. One of them makes breakfast. Mrs. Horrocks comes just before lunchtime, usually.'

'I see. So you were here alone. Did you have any callers or phone calls?'

'No. Nothing.' She indicated three or four of the more expensive sort of women's magazines on a table. 'I was looking at those.'

'So you'll be alone here to-night. Will you be all right? Would you like us to contact any of your friends for you?'

'No. I'll be all right.'

'What about the shop? Will there be someone to take charge?'

'Oh yes. Raymond will look after the shop. Raymond Brotherhood. He's supposed to be the manager.'

'Supposed?'

'Well, Selwyn was such a live wire. I imagine Raymond wouldn't get to do much managing when he was about.'

'I see,' said McCool. He made a note of the name.

Hard Times had returned, and he was sitting where he could see Mrs. Sayle in profile. She turned her head quickly, and caught him staring at her legs with an abstracted air. Neither party was embarrassed.

'I'll be all right,' the woman repeated, 'but I could do with a drink. I'm beginning to feel it now.'

'Allow me,' said Hard Times, springing to his feet and making for the bar. 'What can I get you?'

'Oh, anything. Brandy, I think. With a drop of cold water. And help yourself to whatever you want.'

At the bar Hard Times was behind McCool's back. He found some small balloon glasses and poured two large

26

measures of Courvoisier. He raised one to Mrs. Sayle and drank it quickly. She gave no sign of having noticed the gesture. When she accepted the other glass from him she thanked him without looking at him. He understood perfectly, and grinned behind his wooden expression. He was a man who needed to be kept in his place, he realized. Given half a chance, he would be tapping on her bedroom door. He reflected, without envy, that perhaps she would rather have McCool at her bedroom door.

'Cheers,' she said to McCool, raising the glass a little before she sipped. 'You must think I'm a hard case. I should be swooning and weeping all over the place, I suppose. But it doesn't seem to have taken me that way.'

'Let us hope it never does,' said the inspector. He watched her take another drink, and then he said: 'The safe in Mr. Sayle's downstairs office had been opened. Did he keep anything special in there?'

She gazed at him candidly. 'I have no idea. I know he was up to the top of his head in business affairs, but he never discussed them with me. I know he had a shop and I believe he owned it outright, and that's all I do know. I haven't been in the place more than half a dozen times.'

'Thank you.' He rose to his feet. 'If there is anything else, I'll come and see you again.'

She had put down her glass and risen also. 'Do so, by all means,' she said, apparently with sincerity.

The two detectives departed then, and they heard her lock the outer door behind them. The porch light went out. They strolled along to the garage, which was still brilliantly lighted. On view were a Facel Vega saloon and an open two-seater Jaguar.

'Both hers?' McCool queried.

'Very likely, if Sayle was a Rover man,' Hard Times growled. He walked between the cars and touched their radiators. 'His first wife died of a dog's life, I heard. But there's nothing too good for this one, seemingly.'

There were quick steps on the tarmac. McCool's hand went to the switch on the wall, and the big light died. Then he turned and said 'Hello' in a surprised voice, and put on the lights again. By that time his sergeant had returned to stand beside him.

'Hello,' he said again, to Mrs. Sayle. 'You forgot the garage. We were going to shut it up for you.'

'Thank you,' she said, but her voice was cold. 'I had just remembered it.'

'Two nice cars' he commented, as Hard Times busied himself with the up-and-over doors. 'Both yours?'

'Yes,' she replied. The word was incisive. She did not mind if McCool knew that she was displeased.

They saw her into the house, then they got into the police car and Hard Times drove it away.

'Where's she been this evening?' he asked.

'At home. Since half past six.'

'Five hours ago, nearly. That French car is plenty warm. *Somebody* has had it running since six-thirty.'

4

As the car went down the hill towards the lights of the town, McCool discussed Selwyn Sayle's widow.

'She's sharp,' he said to Hard Times. 'Get that crack she made about the killer being cunning. She got the picture right away. The bad news didn't put her thinking apparatus out of gear. If it *was* bad news.'

Hard Times muttered an insult, but he was referring to the driver behind the blinding headlights which were passing in the opposite direction.

'It's a pity she came out to the garage,' McCool went on. 'You could tell she knew we were snooping.'

'She'll know we know that car was warm.'

'Yes. A pity. We could have had a rummage round in the car.'

'What for? Suppose she dashed off to meet a bloke as soon as her husband had gone to the shop? What's it got to do with us?'

'If that's the case it has everything to do with us. I don't want to miss any moves at the start of this job. Johnny Rodrick is no snip, for my money. I don't see how he could have done it.'

' 'Course he could have done it.'

'Killed Sayle, opened that safe and then gone wandering upstairs among the washing machines?'

'If he had Sayle's keys he went looking for money in the main office.'

'If we find the keys somewhere on the premises I'll grant you that as a possibility. But I still don't think it's feasible. I fancy his mate for it. I'm sure he had a mate.'

'All right. We'll talk to him and get his mate's name. Then to-morrow you can charge the pair of 'em.'

'I hope we can do that, and in the meantime I'm trying to consider all the possibilities, and Mrs. Sayle is one of them.'

'You think she did her old man? What for? She has everything she wants.'

'Including a fellow, if your suggestion is right. He might be a hot-headed young fellow who got tired of waiting for Sayle to have a fatal accident. She might have helped him to arrange this do.'

'Cor!' said Hard Times. 'What a great detective! You and George S. Simenon.'

McCool laughed. 'I'm not talking about probabilities. I'm just bearing in mind what is possible.'

'So how did the fellow get in there?'

'Duplicate key. That would be easy, with Mrs. Sayle's help.'

'Jesus wept,' Hard Times muttered. 'Write a book about it. You'll make a fortune.'

'Come to think of it, why did you feel the radiator of that car?'

'Force of habit. I'm a great detective, too.'

'Well, you certainly started something, didn't you?'

'I'll keep my hands in my pockets in future,' said Hard Times humbly.

'In the meantime, we let Rodrick think he's our choice for the job. We'll make him think we're busy getting him lined up for the assizes. It's the only way to make him sing about his mate.'

'I'm all for that. So what next?'

'This man Brotherhood. If he's gone to bed he'll have to get up. We can't wait till morning.'

They called at Headquarters to get Brotherhood's address from the telephone book. They could have got it from Mrs. Sayle, but that would have been a hint to her that the shop manager was the next person to be interviewed. Perhaps it would not have mattered a great deal, but they had refrained from asking her in pursuance of a sound general policy which they both habitually followed. 'Tell nobody nothing,' was the sergeant's summing-up of it.

Brotherhood lived in White Acre, which was a less opulent suburb than Chestnut Park, and on the other side of the town. Owners lived in Chestnut Park, their managers and under-managers in White Acre. This particular manager occupied a small but fully detached brick box with a garden as tidy and unimaginative as his employer's, but only a fraction of the size. Though the time was getting on towards midnight, the hall light was burning. Also there was a light in a front room downstairs.

McCool rang the bell, and the door was opened by a tall, bony woman about forty years of age. She was a dowdy woman with a thin face and spectacles, and a particularly dowdy hair-do. The hair was straight and dark, scraped back and pinned into a bundle. The scraping and pinning was unsuccessful, because several lank locks had escaped. While she stood with the light behind her they showed clearly, hanging like rats' tails around her head.

The inspector told her that he was from Police Headquarters. 'Are you Mrs. Brotherhood?' he asked.

'I am,' she replied.

'Could I see Mr. Brotherhood? Mr. Raymond Brotherhood?'

The woman seemed to quiver with nervousness or excitement. 'He's gone down to the shop,' she said. 'Mrs. Sayle rang up and told us about poor Mr. Sayle.'

'Thank you,' said McCool. 'Sorry to have disturbed you.' The two men said good night and departed.

In the car Hard Times said: 'So she did phone him after all. Natural enough, I suppose.'

At Sayle's Store a uniformed constable opened the door for them. They went through to Sayle's small office, and found Sergeant Broadhead in conversation with a slim, handsome fellow of medium height, with alert grey eyes, sleek dark hair touched with grey, and a taut mouth. When Broadhead saw Hard Times follow McCool into the room he frowned to show that he disapproved of his opposite number hobnobbing with the inspector when he should have been at home in bed. Hard Times pursed his mouth and blew him a silent raspberry.

'This is Mr. Brotherhead, the manager,' said Broadhead. 'Chief Inspector McCool.'

Brotherhood said: 'How d'you do.' He started to take his right hand from his pocket, then he thrust it back again when the policeman made no move. McCool did not go around shaking hands with everybody when he was working on a case as involved as the present one. He was suspicious of everyone, and he had scruples about shaking hands with people he might have to 'do' later.

But he spoke pleasantly enough. 'We've just been to your house,' he said. 'Mrs. Brotherhood told us you were down here.'

'I haven't been here many minutes,' Brotherhood said. He looked at the floor where Sayle's body had been. 'This is a sad affair.'

McCool reflected that Brotherhood reminded him of somebody. He could not think who it might be. 'Anything missing from the safe?' he asked.

'A cash box which Mr. Sayle kept in there.'

'What was in the cash box? Cash?'

'I don't know. I don't think anybody knows now, except the person who took it. I understood you'd caught the murderer. Hasn't he said anything about it?'

'No. It could be hidden somewhere.' McCool looked at Broadhead.

The sergeant shook his head. 'We found nothing like that. Maffin and Vickery are still looking.'

'It was a mistake for him to take the box,' said Brotherhood. 'He had Mr. Sayle's keys. He could have opened the box, emptied it, and locked it again. Nobody could have proved he'd taken anything.'

'You're assuming there was money in the box?'

'No. I'll say there *might* have been money in it. I work here, you know. I don't want to talk myself into trouble.'

'I see. Well, the man we arrested didn't have the box. And, as you will have gathered, it doesn't seem to be on the premises.'

'In that case there must have been two of them, and the other one got away with the box.'

'Why that particular box?'

'Because it was obviously a cash box, of course. No doubt he felt pushed for time, so he didn't open it and take the contents. If his accomplice had been arrested, he would expect other policemen to arrive at any moment.'

McCool looked at Brotherhood in a manner which suggested that his thoughts were elsewhere. At last he asked: 'Are you thinking that Sayle had already been killed when our man came in and made his arrest?'

'I don't know what to think about that. He could have come in and surprised one of the men, and the other man could have crept up behind him and hit him with the hammer.'

McCool nodded. 'Can you describe the cash box?' he asked.

'It was about eighteen inches by twelve, and about six inches deep. Black metal, with a brass lock.'

'Was it heavy?'

Brotherhood looked at the inspector before he answered.

He smiled faintly. 'I don't know,' he said. 'I never handled it.'

'For the record, would you like to tell me where you'd been this evening?'

'I've been at home all evening.'

'Watching television?'

'I played some records. I don't have television.'

'Congratulations. Were you alone?'

'No. My wife was at home, too.'

'Any callers?'

'No. No phone calls either, until Mrs. Sayle rang.'

'Did you know that Sayle was in the habit of calling at the shop in an evening?'

'Yes. I knew he called occasionally.'

'Did he usually leave his car outside the shop while he was here?'

'I don't know where he left it. I've never been with him when he's visited the shop at night.'

'Where did he usually leave his car when he was here in the daytime?'

'On a bit of spare ground in Herder Street, if he could get on it before it was full.'

'And if he couldn't?'

'He'd leave it outside here till a policeman made him move it. Then he'd put it in the yard. He simply wouldn't pay to put it in a public car park.'

'Why not put it in the yard in the first place?'

'Because it's awkward getting in and out with a three-litre Rover. It's not so bad for a smaller car.'

'Why didn't he leave it across the road in front of the Walnut Tree?'

'He never used that place. He fell out with Mrs. Dennis years ago. I don't know what about.'

'You mean the red-haired woman? The landlady?'

'That's right.'

'He wasn't a popular man, was he?'

'You'll have to ask somebody else about that. I still work here, you know.'

McCool nodded again. 'All right, Mr. Brotherhood,' he said. 'You can go home now. If I need you again I'll get in touch.'

The man said good night and departed. McCool turned to Broadhead. 'Get on the blower and tell them to put out the word on the cash box,' he ordered. 'You know the description.'

Before the sergeant could obey, the telephone rang. McCool reached for it. 'Hello,' he said, and then: 'Speaking.' He listened awhile, then put down the receiver.

'Sayle's car is on that spare ground in Herder Street,' he told the others. 'It's all locked up and there doesn't seem to be anything in it. He could have left it there himself, I suppose.'

.   .   .   .   .

Half an hour later the police quitted Sayle's Store for the night, leaving two constables to watch the place, back and front. McCool and Vickery got into McCool's car, on his instructions. McCool stood with his two sergeants, as they were about to get into another car. He looked almost directly across the street at the Walnut Tree Inn and its wide, deep forecourt. Earlier, when McCool had arrived at Sayle's Store that evening, there had been about a dozen cars on the forecourt. There had been no neon signs and no glaring lights. The windows of the inn had glowed cheerfully but not brilliantly and the forecourt had been in comparative darkness. Now, the inspector's glance was speculative.

Hard Times nudged Broadhead. 'You don't think Mrs. Dennis did it, do you, sir?' he asked.

McCool thought that the idea was ridiculous. He did not say so. He wanted Hard Times to have his fun and talk about Sherlock Holmes and George S. Simenon as much as he liked, because he would eventually have to eat his words. The Sayle murder looked like being a rum job, a very rum job.

McCool knew that Hard Times was under the impression that he was about to be allowed to go home. 'You two must be getting tired,' he said. 'But I'm afraid I have another little job for you. When you get back to Headquarters you'll find a search warrant on Ma Kodrick's place. One of you will have to get his name on it, and then you can go and see what you can find. We mustn't let the grass grow under our feet.'

'And what are you going to do, sir?' Broadhead asked.

'I'm going to have a ding-dong session with Rodrick. Far into the night, if he won't cough.'

'Are you taking those two to help you?' Hard Times queried, nodding towards Maffin and Vickery.

'Those poor lads are in for a long night out of doors. Ah well, it's fine and mild. A lovely night.'

'What are they going to do?'

'I didn't think it was wise to have Brotherhood followed when he left here. But I can stake out his house, and see if he does anything in the dead of night. To-morrow I'm going to put a twenty-four-hour tail on him.'

The two sergeants were astounded. 'For God's sake why?' Broadhead demanded.

McCool grinned, and answered out of the corner of his mouth.

'Ah gotta hunch,' he said.

5

MEN who have served in big police forces are inclined to
say that if they had their time to do again they would do
it in a small, comfortable force, while men who have served
in small forces are likely to say that they would sooner be
in a big force any time. McCool was content to be head of
the C.I.D. in a force of two hundred men, responsible for
clearance of the crime committed in a city with a population
of 110,000. To be in his position, with his rank, at the age
of thirty-six he had done very well. He was young enough
to go elsewhere and attain a much higher rank, but that
would mean administrative work, which he did not like.
He preferred to stay where he was, in the C.I.D. of the
Utterham City Police.

Even the administrative work involved in running an
office with fewer than twenty detectives was a nuisance to
him, and of all his duties the one most likely to be neglected.
He did his best with it, but in the press of other matters
errors of omission in office routine were not uncommon.

So it was that, on the Tuesday morning which followed
the Monday night of Selwyn Sayle's murder, McCool
walked out of the C.I.D. for a conference with Superintendent Sissling, and then remembered that, on a morning
when he was likely to be asked about it, he had not looked
at the duty book. He turned back, and stooped over the
book as it lay on a table in the department's small lobby.
It was this unnoticed return which caused him to overhear

a few remarks by Hard Times, who had his own methods of administration.

The sergeant was addressing Detective Constable Pettit, a young man who liked to keep up with his paper work. He sometimes pottered about in the office when he should have been out in the street, McCool thought.

'Have you ever played cards, Pettit?' Hard Times was asking with heavy geniality.

'Course I have, Sarge. Many a time.'

'Why are all the cards the same on one side?'

'So's you don't know what the other fellow's got.'

'How do you know what you've got yourself?'

'You turn 'em up, o' course. What is all this?'

'What have you got, Pettit?'

'How do you mean, what have I got?'

'You know what I mean. Not poker or pontoon. That Fenner Street job, which you've had on your desk for a fortnight. I'm asking you what you've got.'

'Not much yet, I'm afraid.'

'Well, go and get something. We have some proper cards in this town. Real slippy cards, and all kings and queens till you turn 'em up and find they're knaves. One of 'em did the Fenner Street job. Now get out on to the street and start turning a few up. And while you're about it see if you can find out who Johnny Rodrick's been knocking about with lately.'

McCool closed the duty book and departed at once, so that Pettit on his red-faced emergence would not know that the rough lesson had been overheard. 'That's the stuff,' he mused. 'When a policeman can't take a little nudge like that he's getting too proud for his job.'

He went along to Sissling's office, tapped on the door, and was invited to enter. The superintendent was at his desk, looking at a batch of last night's reports. Physically he was typical of his rank: big, broad, putting on weight, bland when necessary but normally hard of eye. He did not believe in nonsense, nonsense being anything he did not believe in.

'Nice little job last night,' he said without preamble. 'A commendation for Berry, I suppose. It isn't often a P.C. catches a murderer red-handed.'

McCool perceived that the interview was going to be difficult. Well, there would be nothing gained by hedging. 'He wasn't red-handed, and I don't think he's a murderer,' he said.

Sissling stared. 'Nonsense,' he said. 'He broke into the place. He was caught on the premises.'

'True. But he got nothing. Somebody took a cash box off the premises, and it wasn't Rodrick.'

'His china, then. Get him to tell you who it was. Do the pair of 'em.'

'Yes, I think he had a mate. He'll tell me about that, eventually. I hope that'll clear it.'

'You seem doubtful. It's bound to clear it, unless you make a mess of it.'

The superintendent's tone made McCool grow warm. 'And how would I make a mess of it?' he asked softly.

'Now don't start losing your paddy. It was only a manner of speaking. You'll get straight talk from the Chief, you know.'

'The Chief is a gentleman, and you're not,' said McCool, but he did not say it aloud. And actually he did not mean it, because Sissling was basically a very decent fellow. The difference was the Chief was never offensive unless he intended to be, while Sissling could offend without trying.

'I'll give you all the facts I have,' he said, and he gave them. The superintendent listened tolerantly. An imaginary burglar alarm and somebody's hat; a woman who might have a young man on the side and a shop manager whom

McCool had disliked on sight. Really, this was a lot of nonsense.

He was ready with his answers when McCool had finished. 'It's like I said. Get Rodrick's accomplice and your job's cleared. Get 'em accusing each other and that'll be it. The other stuff, it'll all explain itself eventually. Did you flush Rodrick's mother out?'

'I sent Broadhead and Hard Times last night. She hasn't seen him for weeks. He's been living with Vinnie Storr.'

'Well well. There's no telling what a wench will take a fancy to. Have you seen her?'

'Not yet. It's the first job when we've seen the Chief.'

'Buy her some liquor and turn on the charm. She'll tell you who his china was.'

McCool said nothing. He did not need a man who was as subtle as a bull in a field to tell him how to interrogate Virginia Storr. Turn on the charm, my eye! That woman hated policemen. If ever she met a man with good manners she would call him a puff. All she understood was a bottle of gin, a screaming quarrel, a damned good hiding and a reconciliation on the bed. Charm!

'All right, we'll go and see the Chief,' said Sissling.

.   .   .   .   .

'My decision and my responsibility, of course,' said the Chief Constable, squaring his shoulders a little as if the burden were physical. 'But,' he went on, 'I feel that my two most senior officers ought to have a voice in the matter. So, do we call in Scotland Yard?'

Sissling answered promptly. 'We have a man in custody. I don't see that we need the Yard.'

'And your opinion, Chief Inspector?'

McCool spoke carefully. 'I'm not satisfied that the case is cleared, but I don't want the Yard.'

'Well, you know how it is. If we think we're not going to get anywhere with it we call in the Yard. Then if we fail to clear the case critics of the police won't be able to say that we haven't done everything we should have done. Are you sure you can get a conviction for murder?'

'I think I can. I'll go as far as to say that I can get a conviction if anybody can.'

'I'm aware of that, but are the Press and the public aware of it? You know the reputation of the Yard. And there'll be no question of calling them in at a later date when we find we're beaten with the job. If we do that we'll have to pay for their help, and there will be criticism from members of the Finance Committee.'

Sissling spoke up again. 'He'll get his conviction all right if he'll concentrate on what he's got instead of wasting time with extraneous matters.'

'What extraneous matters?' the Chief wanted to know.

'Well, bothering about what Sayle's wife was doing last night, and having the shop manager watched. It's a waste of manpower.'

The Chief looked at McCool with raised eyebrows. McCool took a deep breath, being very near to losing his temper. Sissling's tactless expression of an opinion seemed at that moment to be a deliberate attempt to belittle the head of the C.I.D. in front of the Chief. Even Hard Times had been more considerate with Pettit. He had at least waited until he thought he was alone with the man.

The thought of Pettit eased the situation for McCool. He even managed a taut grin. That was the way of the world, the top dogs saying what they liked and the underdogs having to be careful. He coolly considered his answer, and gave it.

'At the moment I'm in charge of the Sayle case,' he said. 'I'm trying to cover it thoroughly and properly. That is my way of doing things. If I'm not going to be allowed to work

41

in my own way I respectfully suggest that I'm taken off the job and someone else put in charge.'

'Now then,' said Sissling. 'I was only saying what I thought.'

'I can't criticize thoroughness, even if it does sometimes appear to be wasteful,' said the Chief. 'You've convinced me, Chief Inspector. You can handle the job in your own way, and the best of luck to you. We'll take our chances and do without Scotland Yard.'

That was the end of the conference for McCool, and he received the Chief's permission to depart. When he had gone, Sissling said thoughtfully: 'He's been up all day and all night, more or less. No wonder he's a bit touchy.'

The Chief thought that McCool had shown admirable restraint. 'I wish I had a hundred like him,' he said tersely.

.   .   .   .   .

The Stipendiary Magistrate had remanded Johnny Rodrick in custody on the shop-breaking charge, following a police request for time to make further inquiries into that and other matters. Everybody knew about the 'other matters', because the news of Sayle's murder had been in all the morning papers. Rodrick knew also. McCool was very carefully keeping him under the impression that he would eventually be charged with the murder. That was not the only way to soften him into betrayal of an accomplice, but it was the one which seemed to be the most expedient.

Leaving Rodrick to worry in his cell, McCool went with Hard Times to see Virginia Storr. The sergeant knew that the girl lived somewhere in Hatters Causeway, a street of dwellings which had seen better days, but not much better. Premises which had housed poor but hard-working families now gave shelter to shifty migrants whose only luggage was a comb and a pair of socks, and to thieves and women of ill repute who lived in rooms described as 'furnished'. The furniture was mainly of the sort which can be acquired after any auction for the trouble of taking it away. The entire street was due for demolition.

In Hatters Causeway McCool lowered the window of the car and spoke to three slatternly women who were talking on a corner. 'Where does Vinnie Storr live?' he asked.

The women looked at each other. They seemed to make a tacit agreement that this was a matter upon which they might give information to two detectives.

'Number eleven,' one of them said. 'But you won't find her at home.'

'She's just gone up the street,' said another with a sly flash of false teeth. 'They're open.'

McCool looked at his watch. The time was eleven-forty. The public houses had opened ten minutes ago.

'Which one does she use?' he asked.

'The nearest,' the third woman said drily.

McCool thanked them. Hard Times prepared to turn the car. 'Shall we try the Beagle?' he asked.

At the Beagle Inn they entered by the back door, and caught a glimpse of Vinnie in the saloon bar. The snug behind the bar was deserted at that time of day. They entered the tiny room and sat down. McCool rang the bell.

The landlord appeared. He made them welcome. There was no profit for him in being surly with the police, and in any case those two were not enemies of his. It was the men of the uniformed police and not the C.I.D. who exerted themselves to enforce the licensing laws.

'Two bitters, please,' said McCool. 'And would you tell Miss Storr that two gentlemen would like to see her in the snug?'

The landlord was amused. 'I'll do that,' he said.

Miss Storr arrived before the beer. She entered the room

looking bright and expectant, a girl who was attractive and apparently healthy in spite of a degenerate way of life. Her smile died instantly when she saw the two men, and her lip curled in disgust.

'Two gentlemen? Two bloody coppers!' she exclaimed.

She turned with the intention to depart, but the landlord, with a tray, was just entering the room. McCool stretched a long arm and caught hers. He nodded to Hard Times, and the sergeant grasped the girl by the waist with two hands, and forced her to sit on the bench beside him.

'What's your hurry?' he growled, grinning at her.

'Take your clumsy hands off me,' she snapped.

'Be quiet,' said McCool. 'What would you like to drink?'

She stared at him in astonishment. 'You're buying me one?'

'I've just made the offer.'

She grinned. 'In that case I'll have a gin. A big one.'

McCool spoke to the landlord. 'Please bring this woman a small gin, and as much water as she requires.'

'I'll have a tonic with it, you skinny devil,' said Vinnie. 'What are you after? Is it Johnny?'

'Why should it be Johnny?'

'Well, he didn't come home last night, so I expect he's been locked up. Coppers don't come in pairs for the other job. They'll be coming to see me if you put Johnny in the nick.'

McCool did not cease to smile. He said: 'If I catch any of my lads messing about with you I'll have him off the force so quick he won't have time to pick his hat up.'

'They'll be around,' she said. 'Platoons of 'em. I've had bobbies before.'

'You've had *one* bobby before,' he corrected her. 'He was a fool for anything in high heels. He isn't with us any more.'

'You don't know it all.'

'You'd be surprised. But I didn't come here to discuss

your connections with the force. Johnny's in real trouble. You might be able to help him.'

Her smile mocked him. 'By talking to you?'

'Don't you want to help him?'

'I couldn't care less.'

'You were living with him, weren't you?'

'He was living with me. I let him stay at my place. I don't owe him a thing. He didn't even pay the rent.'

'So you told him to go out and get some money, and he went and broke in Sayle's Store.'

'Is that what he did? Bloody fool.'

'He was arrested on the premises, and Selwyn Sale was found murdered.'

Her eyes widened and she put a hand to her mouth. 'Murder?' she gasped.

'Haven't you seen a paper this morning?'

She shook her head. 'Murder,' she muttered. 'He did a murder.'

'You knew he was going to do the Sayle job, didn't you?'

'No, I didn't.' She was alert again. 'You don't drag me into no murder case.'

'I'll drag you into nothing you aren't in already. But you don't want to let Johnny take all the humpy, do you? We both know he wasn't the only one, don't we?'

'I don't know what you're talking about.'

'I think you do. Who was Johnny's mate for the job?'

'I don't know. I don't know anything about it.'

'Where is your brother these days? He's good enough for a murder.'

'Our Micky had nothing to do with it. He was at home. I was there too, so I know.'

'Are you trying to tell me Mick never went out last night?'

'Yes, I am. And there's me and my mother to prove it.'

'I thought you and your mother couldn't agree.'

'We can agree on that at any rate.'

'How long is it since either you or Micky stayed out of a pub for an entire evening? Ten years?'

'Our Micky stayed in last night, and I'll bear witness to it.'

'That settles it, then,' said McCool with sarcasm. 'But if Mick wasn't with Johnny, who was?'

'Happen he was on his own.'

'You know better. And if we don't find out who was with him he'll have to stand for it himself. It's a hanging job, you know.'

He was watching her closely. Though she looked defiant he could see that his words troubled her, and he was unable to decide whether her anxiety was on behalf of Johnny, or her brother, or someone else. But her attitude made him fairly certain of one thing—that she was not yet ready to give him any information.

'I have a search warrant for your place,' he said. 'Do you want to be present when we search?'

She was pert. 'What for? You'll find naught. You can have my key if you want.'

She took a latchkey from her handbag and put it on the table. McCool picked it up. 'I'll leave it in the door,' he said, rising to his feet.

The two detectives left the inn. As they were getting into the car Hard Times remarked: 'She was much too obliging with that key.'

'Yes. It's so transparent it makes you wonder if there's more to it. We go and search her room while she nips round to her mother's and fixes Mick's alibi.'

They both knew very well where Micky Storr lived. They went there, and met his mother just as she was leaving the house with a basket full of empty bottles.

'Hello there, Mrs. Storr,' McCool called from the car. 'How are you?'

'I'm as well as I deserve to be,' she replied. 'Who are you after this time?'

'How's Mick these days?' ,

'Same as he always is.'

'Is he at home?'

'No. He'll be in for his dinner at three, not before. He can't manage to get home before the pubs shut. What's he been doing?'

'I'm not saying he's been doing anything. I just wanted a word with him.'

'Well, he'll be home at three.'

'I hear he's taken to staying in of a night.'

'He's never stayed in of a night since he could toddle.'

'He was out last night, then?'

'I've always told him I'd never lie to get him out of his scrapes, so it's no comment.'

'How's your Vinnie going on?'

'I haven't seen that little bitch in a month,' the woman said incisively, 'and it'll suit me if I don't see her in a twelvemonth.'

6

McCool spoke to Headquarters on his car radio, to the
effect that Michael Storr was 'wanted for interview'. Then
he went with Hard Times to search Vinnie's room. That
was a brief task. An unscrubbed floor without carpet can
not be disturbed without leaving unmistakable signs, and
neither can worn upholstery or an ancient mattress. The
two men found nothing of interest.

They returned to the office and found that Micky had
already been picked up. He was waiting in the C.I.D.
under the eye of the detective officer who had brought him
in. He was jaunty and unworried, a strong, tough little
man with a battered nose, and a black eye which was
much worse than Rodrick's.

'I'm laughing,' he said to McCool. 'As long as you don't
keep me here till closing time I'm happy. I haven't been
near Sayle's Store for a month, and I can prove it.'

'Just prove you weren't there last night,' said McCool.
'That's all I ask.'

Micky grinned. He produced Woodbines and matches,
and smoked with an air of pensive contentment.

'Well, go on,' said McCool. 'Give us your alibi.'

'Haha. It couldn't be better if I'd arranged it. I was
playing at dominoes in the taproom at the Star from
eight o'clock till half past ten. I never left the table except
for one call, one minute, at the Gents. I usually move on
from there at nine o'clock, but I kept winning and having

a pint to come, and before I'd supped it I'd won another. I never lost a game.'

'How did you get the shiner?'

'I played a wrong domino. Some blokes is a bit hasty, like.'

'Name your witnesses at the Star.'

Micky rattled off half a dozen names. He had them ready. He had already recited them to the officer who had picked him up.

McCool looked at the officer. 'Have you had time to verify any of that?'

'Not yet, sir.'

'Go and do so, now. When you're satisfied, ring in and we can let him go.'

The man departed. McCool turned to Micky. 'Did you see anything of Johnny Rodrick last night?'

'No. Nor the night before. I haven't seen Rodrick for long enough.'

'He's a pal of yours, isn't he?'

'And living on my sister? I should say not!'

'Who are his pals?'

'He hasn't got any.'

'He must have. Everybody has a friend somewhere.'

'You'll have a job on to find any friend of that monkey.'

'Who does he drink with?'

'His self. Or our Vinnie.'

'Vinnie has friends, hasn't she? He must mix with them.'

'The sort of men friends Vinnie has, they don't want to be with her when she's with Rodrick. And the sort of women friends she has, they keep their blokes out of her way, in case she takes a fancy to 'em.'

'Have you seen *anybody* with Rodrick recently?'

'No, I can't say as I have.'

'Anyway, your sister thought there was half a chance you were with Rodrick. She tried to give you an alibi.'

Ah,' said Micky approvingly. 'Just in case, happen. She's a good kid.'

That was the end of the interview. McCool went into his own office shaking his head. He still believed that Rodrick had not been alone at Sayle's. He had been checking. Never in his life had Rodrick committed a crime without an accomplice. He was one of those men who did not have the courage to work alone.

.   .   .   .   .

By means of a submersible magnet, the cash box from Selwyn Sayle's private safe was found in the River Utter. It was open, and empty. The police tried under and over, as they say in that part of England, to ascertain whether it had contained money, and if so, how much. The murdered man's diary was strictly a business document. It contained plenty of figures, and all of them could be connected with the matters to which they were related. None of them referred to the cash box. There was no mention of it in his personal papers or in his will. His widow had not even known of its existence. No past or present employee had . ever seen it opened. Now that Sayle was dead, nobody knew what the box had contained: except, of course, the man who had taken it and emptied it.

'It's a hell of a position,' said McCool. 'If we caught some little tea-leaf with five thousand pounds under his bed, we wouldn't know for certain it had come from that box.'

'Unless we made him cough,' said Hard Times.

'Would you cough with five thousand in the kitty, and nobody able to prove where you'd got it from?'

'And the only reward for talking, a special fitting for a Pentonville necktie? No, I don't think I'd divulge the information.'

'There's nobody terribly keen on having the job cleared,

either. Mrs. Sayle doesn't seem to care, and that fellow Brotherhood is about as much help as a housemaid's knee. He's gone into his shell, and all he can say is that he doesn't want to stick his neck out. A remarkably vivid phrase in the circumstances, I will admit.'

Hard Times shrugged tolerantly. Police observations on Brotherhood had not yet produced any information, and in his opinion they never would. Neither could he see any chance of profit in McCool's 'research' on Mrs. Sayle, though he had hopes that it would uncover a spicy situation. Every man in the Utterham Police now had the number and description of the lady's Jaguar. They did not need the number of her Facel Vega, because it was the only car of that make in the town. Perhaps more than anybody the police make use of that development of modern life which enables some of the habits and movements of people to be known by knowing their cars.

'You suspect everybody, don't you?' Hard Times said.

'I do,' was the terse reply. 'I wouldn't trust the Pope's uncle if he was mixed up in this job.'

'It just makes work for all of us,' the sergeant said, with resignation.

'Well, you've nothing better to do. Look here, I want to talk to somebody on the inside of Sayle's Store. I see Joe Wakeley's name on this staff list. Would he be any good to us?'

'I don't know. We could try him.'

'Any idea who got him the job?'

'I did.'

McCool nodded. In their own way, unofficially, policemen work for the rehabilitation of criminals. They are suitable men for this work because they are not easily fooled. They know their 'clients', and have a better idea than anybody when a man is really trying to put the past behind him and live an honest and useful life.

Joe Wakeley had emerged from Dartmoor three years earlier, after serving half a lifetime in prison. His last five-year sentence had finally broken his heart. 'I can't stand that place like I useter,' he had complained to Hard Times. 'Another lagging in there 'ud kill me. I'm that full of rheumatics you wouldn't believe.'

'So you can't run up and down fall pipes any more,' the sergeant commented with satisfaction.

'It isn't that. I just daren't take a chance on going back. I'm not going to be bent any more. True blue, me. As soon as I can get a job.'

'Have you tried?'

'Yers. The welfare folk have tried, an' all. No luck yet. It's my record, such a bad 'un. And I wouldn't accept work without telling I'm a gaolbird. I'd never be comfortable that way. It 'ud be as bad as having done a sloppy screwing job and waiting for a copper to come and feel your collar.'

'So,' said Hard Times to McCool three years later, 'I got him this job at Sayle's, and told him if he nicked as much as a handful of nails I'd get him ten P.D. So far he hasn't been caught doing anything. I think he's been a good boy.'

'Right. He may not know a lot, but he can put us on to somebody who does know. You'd better get him here.'

'I'd better not approach him in working hours. How about to-night?'

'That'll do very well,' said McCool.

At seven o'clock that evening Wakeley entered the C.I.D. in some trepidation. McCool did not try to put him at ease. He would do that when he had got all the information which the man could give.

'Do you know Johnny Rodrick?' he began.

'Sure I know him. I mean, I know of him.'

'Ever had any dealings with him?'

'No. I was doing bird all the time he was coming up.

And what I've heard of him I wouldn't touch him with the long tackle.'

'Where were you on Monday night?'

'I was at home, watching the telly.'

'Anybody with you?'

'Only the wife. For God's sake, Mr. McCool, you're not going to pull me into this murder job, are you? Me with my record? I know I've been on the crook all my life, but I never roughed anybody. An old man of eighty could've put the arm on me if he caught me right. If Rodrick had a mate, it wasn't me. For the last three years I haven't put a foot wrong. That's God's honest truth, sir.'

'I understand the sergeant here got you your job at Sayle's.'

'Yes, he did. He always treated me right. Well, all the coppers did, I must admit. I never went down for summat I didn't do.'

McCool looked at the police-prison fear in Wakeley's eyes, and he felt very sorry for the man. But he did not show his pity.

He asked: 'Was Mr. Brotherhood the manager at Sayle's when you started there?'

'No. Brotherhood was only a understrapper at the time. Fred Talbot was the manager, and a nice gentleman too. He had a bit of kindness in his heart for a man who was down. I found out, some time after, as when the sergeant ast him to help me he fairly had to beg Mr. Sayle to give me a chance, and the morning I started work Sayle came into the packing room and spoke to me very severe. He said he was going to keep an eye on me. He always looked at me very suspicious, and he's never give me a civil word all the time I've worked for him. But that don't mean I'd aught to do with murdering him.'

'Did Fred Talbot retire?'

'No. Don't you remember? He fell in the river and got

drowned, poor man. I trembled for my job for a while after that.'

'I remember,' said McCool. He remained in thought for a little while, and then he said: 'So Brotherhood got Mr. Talbot's job? What sort of a boss is he?'

'Well, I don't have nothing to do with him. Osbert the packing-room foreman is my boss. So long as I don't get across with Osbert, Mr. Brotherhood doesn't know I exist.'

'And what does Osbert say about Mr. Brotherhood?'

'Osbert's a foreman, you understand. What he thinks about the boss he keeps to hisself.'

'I understand. What did Osbert think about Mr. Talbot?'

'Osbert thought Mr. Talbot was a gentleman, and he said so many a time.'

'But he never says Mr. Brotherhood is a gentleman?'

'He never says anything at all about Mr. Brotherhood.'

'Did Osbert ever say that Mr. Sayle was a gentleman?'

'No, he never did. Mr. Sayle has said some very rough things to him at different times, in front of the men.'

'What's his full name?'

'Osbert Hatton. He's all right, but don't say I as much as mentioned his name.'

'That's all right. Anything you say here is confidential. Nobody will even know you've been talking to me, unless you spill it yourself.'

'Don't fret yourself, I'll spill nothing,' said Wakeley fervently. He was relieved. 'You only had me here to get some chat about the firm?'

'That's right. The sergeant helped you, and I thought you might be kindly disposed.'

'Well, I am an' all. So long as I'm in the clear.'

'Nobody's in the clear till the job's wrapped up.'

'Well, I realize that. But you don't specially suspect me?'

'No, we don't suspect you. I'd like to get a line into the office at Sayle's.'

'I can't help you. I've never been in the office. It's on the top floor, and the packing room is on the ground floor at the back, so I can't get a line nowhere like that.'

'The fellows in the office, what is their favourite spot for a drink?'

'There aren't any fellows in the office, only Brotherhood. He's got a harem up there. The only fellows are the counter-jumpers in the ironmongery, because they understand tools, the packing-room staff, and the delivery men. There are girls on all the other floors, and women in charge of 'em. Happen Brotherhood will get hisself a male assistant now that Sayle's gone, but I don't know about that.'

McCool picked up the personnel list and looked at it, and he perceived that Wakeley's information was correct.

'As you say, Brotherhood has a harem. He's the right lad for it, from the look of him. Handsome fellow.'

'Look,' said Wakeley, becoming anxious again. 'He's my boss. He can sack me just like that. What are you wanting to talk about him for, anyway?'

'Oh, just routine. I've got to get all the information I can, you know. Do the girls like him?'

'Some of 'em do, from what I hear.'

'And does he like the girls?'

Wakeley shrugged.

'Have you ever heard of him having any dealings with a girl outside of office hours?'

'Look, I don't get this at all. What are you after exactly?'

'A woman scorned. An old flame who might give me a line into that office.'

'You don't want none of the girls, they're too young mostly. I'll give you a name, and when I go out of here that name has never passed my lips.'

'Fair enough.'

'This is only rumour what I've heard. The name is Mrs. Reed, boss of the third floor.'

'Thanks, and don't worry, Joe. Does Brotherhood take a drink?'

'I've seen him go into the Walnut Tree across the road from the shop. That's why I never go in there. It's not my sort of pub anyway. Even the taproom company is posh.'

'Does Mrs. Reed go in there?'

'I don't know. I think I've told you enough.'

'Possibly you have. Thanks again, and you can go. Good night.'

Wakeley departed. McCool said: 'It's a shame to upset the old boy, but we've got to get our information where we can.'

Hard Times said nothing. His manner indicated that the whole thing was a waste of time in his opinion.

McCool went on: 'That drowning. Fred Talbot. Who was Coroner's Officer at that time?'

'Oh dear,' said Hard Times wearily. 'Here we go again. What's the use of bringing that up?'

'I asked you, who handled that job?'

'It wasn't exactly a job. What was done, I did it. Fred Talbot was a dear old friend of mine, and when I saw the Sudden Death report I just made sure nobody made a mess of it.'

'In what way could that have been done?'

'You know how people talk. For the sake of his good name I didn't want the slightest suspicion of suicide—unless it *was* suicide.'

'And wasn't it?'

'There was no evidence of it. There was some evidence of an accident.'

'Tell me about it.'

Hard Times sighed. He knew quite well what was behind that sharp, terse manner. Another stray suspicion had found its way into McCool's head. Now he was going to make a mystery over poor old Fred Talbot.

'Well,' the sergeant began, 'Fred used to go to the Ship Inn nearly every night and have a quiet hour in the snug with a few of his old chums. When it was wet he used to come and go on the bus, and when it was fine he used to walk along the river bank. This particular night he went to the Ship on the bus, but when he came out it had stopped raining and he decided to walk. The river was high, and running fast. He was seen by two of his friends to set off along the river road at twenty to eleven, and he wasn't seen again till they fished him out of the water the day after, down at Kingsborough. It was the damnedest thing.'

'What was?'

'At the bend by the hospital wall the stonework of the river bank had washed away, and some kids had smashed the street light there. There was more rain threatening, and the sky was as black as the inside of a coal bunker. Without a light, and with all those trees, it would be real dark just there. We had to assume that Fred fell into the river at the place where the banking was broken, because he couldn't see it. It was the only explanation.'

'And you found nothing to contradict that theory?'

'No. Not a thing.'

'What was the condition of the body when he was found? Any injuries?'

'Plenty, but none inflicted before his death by drowning.'

'Were all his possessions, money and so forth, still in his pockets?'

'Yes. There was nothing taken that I could see.'

'Could he swim?'

'Yes, but he was turned sixty and not in the best of condition. And as I told you, the river was in spate.'

'What about the liquor he'd had?'

'Ah, there's the rub. He liked a drop, did Fred. At the inquest all his old drinking pals said he'd had only three pints of beer, and was sober. But one of 'em told me in confidence that he'd had six or seven pints, and was moderately merry.'

'Did he often drink so much?'

'Quite often, I believe. But he could carry it.'

'Did many people know of his habit of walking along the riverside?'

'Everybody who knew him, I should think.'

'H'm. And Brotherhood inherited his job at Sayle's. Did you ever find the kids who had busted the street light?'

'No. I tried, just to round the job off. But I couldn't get anybody to own to it.'

'Did it ever occur to you that these kids—if it was kids—might also have helped the river bank to get itself broken down?'

Hard Times put a hand to his head. It was as he had feared. Now McCool suspected that Fred Talbot had been murdered. He was on the trail, with his nose down. Him and Agatha Christie.

7

Mc Cool liked to drink occasionally, and the Walnut Tree Inn was his sort of pub. Nevertheless, he did not openly approach the place and walk in. He needed to go in there apparently by accident, with an acquaintance. So he took up a position in the shadowed alleyway beside Sayle's Store, and he watched from there. The time of night was nine o'clock, a reasonable hour for a moderate drinker, by English standards.

He had been there for only ten minutes when he saw the man who would, unsuspecting, serve his purpose. Wally Hunter was the manager of a small local branch of a big building society. He was a native of the town, and closely or distantly he knew everybody who was worth knowing and nobody who was not. McCool came into the category of those worth knowing because he was chief inspector of police.

Wally was on foot, according to his habit when he was going for a drink. McCool gauged his speed nicely. He emerged from the entry, crossed the street diagonally, and appeared to be happily surprised when Wally hailed him.

'Hello, Jim,' said the building society man, because James was McCool's given name. 'What are you doing? Looking for sixpences? You'll never catch a thief that way.'

'I was deep in thought, Wally. How are you?'

'I'm moderately fit, thanks. And you?'

'I'm up to the eyes in work. I've got it round my neck.'

That calculated remark was successful. Wally's shrewd glance swept across the street to Sayle's and back again. He was curious, about the murder of a man he knew. Also, other men were curious, and the ability to gossip with authority and inside knowledge was a social asset. And here was McCool, the man in charge of the investigation. A man worth knowing.

'Come and refresh yourself at this nearby hostelry,' he said. 'Give yourself an hour off.'

McCool hesitated. He was seen to weaken. He said: 'I may have time for the odd one.'

'Sure you have,' was the hearty rejoinder.

The two men entered the pleasant lounge bar of the inn. The Walnut Tree was one of the oldest buildings in the city. It had recently been altered to comply with modern requirements, but the alterations had been carried out with taste and discretion. Strangers, and especially Americans, Australians and Canadians, were apt to say that it was delightful. Its chief merit in the eyes of local people was that it was a free house which sold good liquor and attracted decent company.

'I'm having a pint of Whitbread,' said Wally. 'What's yours?'

'The same.'

'Good. Two pints of you-know-what, Peggy.'

Peggy was a haughty beauty, but Wally was a prosperous regular and McCool was unmarried, good-looking and successful. She served them with a smile.

They quaffed. They talked around the edge of things, lightly, without much thought. McCool glanced casually along the bar, then he leaned with his back to it and looked over the customers sitting at tables. He saw Raymond Brotherhood. And, with a feeling of impending embarrassment, he saw Josephine Tavenant.

Jo was sitting at a table with Brotherhood. Somehow that was no surprise to McCool. He knew her well. She was the only girl he had ever wanted to marry. He still carried the ring she had returned to him. It was his luck piece, a token of a fortunate escape.

'Why should I be bothered about her?' he asked himself. She was the one who had done the jilting. And it had happened ten years ago. As far as he was concerned, she was now the merest acquaintance.

'I see you've spotted Brotherhood,' Wally murmured. 'He's dropped right on his feet, with this job.'

'You mean, he has the running of the shop?'

'That's right. And it's not only that. He's already seeing this fellow and the other fellow.'

McCool perceived that a quite usual thing was happening. Wally had invited him to have a drink with the object of getting information, and was now proceeding to give it.

'This fellow and that fellow? Do you mean he's trying to form a syndicate of backers?'

'We'll say that's your guess, old boy. You said it, not me. There's many a widow been swindled because she didn't know the value of what she'd inherited.'

'A syndicate to buy the business, with Brotherhood advising the widow? Is that it?'

'If it is so—I say if it's so—he's not wasting much time, is he? But that sort of business has to be done quickly, if anybody is going to make any money.'

'Surely the widow will take other advice. She'll have her own lawyer.'

'Who may not know the value of the business. Who may not even want to know. Wheels within wheels, you know. There may be some influential men interested.'

'But such a syndicate would probably sell out and take a quick profit if they got the shop cheap. And then where would Brotherhood be?'

'Sitting pretty, or I don't know the man. By Jove, I wonder . . .'

Wally looked at Jo Tavenant, and closed his mouth. McCool wondered also. What new surmise had occurred to Wally? Something about Jo and the man who was with her? Was that a thoroughgoing affair, or just a chance meeting of friends? 'I'm damned if I care,' said McCool to himself.

Then Wally's sly glance made McCool aware that he had remembered the story of Jo Tavenant's marriage. Jo Joynson she had been, and a smart, smart girl. She was secretary to Lionel Tavenant, a wealthy machine-tool man, and engaged to McCool, who was no bigger than a detective constable at that time. Tavenant's wife had run off with an even wealthier machine-tool man, and a divorce had followed. Then Tavenant, newly unmarried, found that his delightful secretary was not as unapproachable as he had thought. He was a susceptible man, and she hooked him, played him and gaffed him with expert ease. And about that time the unsuspecting McCool received a registered package, containing his ring and a sweet, regretful letter.

In the three years of his second marriage Tavenant gradually realized that Jo did not love him as much as she had vowed she did. He was an easy-going man. He shrugged, and wandered off into the reach of a rich widow who landed him as easily as Jo had done. The widow was a person of such terrific local standing and influence that, once Tavenant had been seduced by her, his divorce and remarriage to her followed as a matter of course. But so great a person was she that it was not considered proper for her to be cited as co-respondent. Another, nominal, adultress, had been found, and with her Tavenant had 'provided the evidence'.

Long before Tavenant was ready to present her with his

false evidence, wily Jo had secured the real evidence, in which the widow was deeply involved. The word 'blackmail' was never mentioned, but when the divorce went through on the false evidence, the settlement made out of court was, as McCool now recalled, nobody's business. Josephine Tavenant was, financially, very comfortable. And her good name was untarnished. Among the people who were her friends, opportunism and hard bargaining were never blameworthy.

Since being jilted by Jo, McCool had never contemplated marriage. That could have been significant, but it was not. There had been other women in his life after Jo. They had not been hard to find nor, since he had never actually fallen in love, hard to leave behind. Since Jo, he had never led a girl into serious thought of marriage. He was not only free, he had a clear conscience.

With regard to Jo, his only regret was that he had never succeeded in anticipating the wedding night with her. That would have been something to balance the duplicity and disappointment of the final days of their engagement. He could look at her now without resentment, and indeed without any feeling at all. He saw her as a woman who was as beautiful and attractive as ever, but his appraisal was impersonal.

'Thinking of the old days?' Wally ventured.

'No,' said McCool shortly. 'There's too much in the present time to think about.'

'You'll have been busy on Selwyn Sayle's murder.'

'Yes.'

'Looking for more evidence against this man Rodrick, I suppose?'

'Trying to make a tidy parcel of the job.'

'What a thing to happen to a man, in his own shop. You might almost call it rough justice.'

'Didn't you like him?'

'Did anybody? He was unspeakable. The way he treated his first wife! The doctor advised a house at the seaside for her, then a long sea voyage, then a holiday at least. She got damn all. Sayle said he couldn't afford it. The mannerless, heartless, penny-pinching huckster!'

'He hasn't pinched many pennies with the new wife.'

'I should say not. A new house and a Facel Vega, not to mention a sports Jag. He must have been besotted.'

'Do you know her, his widow?'

'No. In a slight sort of way I wish I did.'

'Why?'

'Business, my dear chap. I'm in the money business and she's going to inherit plenty of it.'

'I see. I've met her, of course. She seems to be a level-headed sort of person.'

'She'll need to be, I think.'

McCool nodded absently. He was studying Jo and her companion. They were deep in conversation, and had not yet seen him. He reflected that they were a handsome couple. Like Mrs. Sayle, Jo was a blonde. Physically and mentally, he thought, the two women were of the same type. Following a careful comparison, Jo would perhaps have been judged the better-looking of the two. She had a small but perfect figure, a perfect skin and obviously perfect health. She looked well in white, and often wore it. Now she was wearing a loose white coat which looked expensive, and probably was. Brotherhood was an ideal partner for her, with his good but not beefy shoulders, his dark hair with a touch of grey, and the sort of slightly satanic face which always attracts women. McCool again wondered whose likeness he saw in that face. Not the devil's, somebody else's.

'Nice, isn't she?' Wally remarked. 'I don't think she's seen you yet.'

'No, she's busy. Is she often with that fellow?'

'I don't want to be a witness to anything.'

'Bless you, you won't be. The police don't meddle in marital affairs.'

'I've seen them together a number of times. They seem to meet here.'

'And depart together, or separately?'

'Sometimes the one, sometimes the other. He's a bit of a lad, is Brotherhood. He had another wench in tow not so long ago. One of the women from the shop. A big redhead.'

'Married woman?'

'I don't know. I believe they call her Helen Reed.'

'Does she still come in here?'

'Not now. She goes into the Puzzle Bar in the Horse-market. At least, I've seen her there with another woman. I've heard talk about her, but I've never seen her with a man, except the gentleman you're looking at.'

'Thanks, Wally,' said McCool. He ordered two more pints of beer and turned his back on Jo and Brotherhood. He thought that it would be a good idea if he departed without being seen by them. He would go and look for Helen Reed in the Puzzle Bar.

He drank his beer without undue haste. A glance at Jo left him with the impression that he still had not been noticed. He murmured a good night to Wally, smiled at the barmaid and departed. Outside, he breathed deeply to get the tavern air out of his lungs, then crossed the road and walked along Commonside towards the street where he had left his car.

About a hundred yards away from the Walnut Tree a sports car was standing at the kerb, and behind it stood a small two-door saloon. There were two women in the saloon. McCool glanced at them as he passed. They did not seem to notice him, because they were both staring intently in the direction of the inn. When he was a little way past the car he turned to get a better look. The woman in the seat next to the driver's had a profile which was vaguely familiar. He felt almost sure that she was Mrs. Brotherhood.

He walked on to his car and drove back towards the Walnut Tree. As he went he spoke on the radio to the operator at Headquarters, and asked: 'Find out who's in the C.I.D., will you?'

'Maffin for one, sir,' the man said. 'I've just seen him go through.'

'Maffin will do. Get him at once, please. Tell him I'll be waiting in my car on Commonside, this side of Sayle's Store. Tell him to hurry.'

By the time he had finished giving his orders he was pulling in to the kerb in Commonside, about two hundred yards behind the saloon with the female occupants. He waited there. In two or three minutes Maffin opened the door of the car and slipped in beside him. He was breathing rather hard.

'Something doing?' he asked.

'That little Austin up there. Two women in it, keeping observations with binoculars. Night glasses, maybe.'

'Observations on what?'

'One of them is Mrs. Brotherhood, and the other one looks as if she might be her sister. Mr. B. is in the Walnut Tree, with a lady. I know that's none of our business, but something of interest might come out of it.'

'Something for us, sir?'

'Possibly. A row. Words spoken in the heat of the moment, and afterwards regretted.'

Far ahead a white convertible moved out of the Walnut Tree forecourt into the bright lights of Commonside.

'There goes the lady, I think,' said McCool. 'I wonder if she's alone.'

A dark-coloured saloon of medium size followed the convertible, and immediately the Austin began to move also. McCool started his car and joined the procession.

'Any chance of them noticing us?' was Maffin's reasonable query.

'Those two? I think not. So long as we drive with sidelights we can follow them from here to Halifax and they won't see us. Brotherhood might spot *them*, but we can't help that.'

Suddenly the Austin's tail lights grew brighter. 'They're stopping at Regency Terrace,' said Maffin.

'Yes,' McCool agreed. 'The other two cars will have turned along there.' He did not decrease speed, but went on past the Austin. A woman had alighted and turned the corner into Regency Terrace, and the car was moving again.

'Now the Austin's following us,' Maffin commented, looking back.

McCool kept going, and turned off the main road when he was several streets further along. He drove fast to come round to the other end of Regency Terrace. The Austin continued along the main road.

There were a number of cars standing in Regency Terrace, but Jo's white convertible was unmistakable. McCool stopped his own car some distance away from it, and on the other side of the street. He could see a car standing behind the convertible, and that was probably Brotherhood's.

The elegant town houses of Regency Terrace had nearly all been made into roomy and expensive flats, four flats to each house. The one in which Jo appeared to live showed lights on all four floors. Everybody was at home, apparently. The glow from the windows of the ground-floor flat shone on the upturned face of the only person in sight, the woman whom McCool took to be Mrs. Brotherhood. She moved into the light from the doorway, and stood looking at nameplates.

'I'm surprised she hasn't brought her sister along as a witness,' Maffin remarked.

'That's a clue to the poor lady's attitude. She's not seeking evidence for a divorce. She just wants to stop her husband's larking around.'

'So she won't hang about to give them time to get cracking.'

'No. She won't be able to bear that. She'll make up her mind in a minute and barge straight in.'

As he spoke, Mrs. Brotherhood climbed the four steps to the open doorway and disappeared.

'So she'll fetch him out in a minute,' said Maffin.

'There'll be a certain amount of straight talk first,' McCool guessed. 'I'd like to hear it.'

He opened the door of the car. 'Take over,' he said. 'Drive on and stop a hundred yards past the door.'

He went to the house and looked at the nameplates. They were arranged vertically, and Jo's name was the second from the bottom. So she lived one flight up, and the stairs were well lighted. That made eavesdropping a chancy business. McCool wondered if it was worth the risk. He did not want Brotherhood to see him and become aware of police interest.

He moved suddenly as there was the click of a ball-catch. The door of the ground-floor flat was opened. A woman emerged. 'I won't be long, dear,' she said. She closed the door of the flat and appeared on the steps of the house. McCool was quite near, but walking towards her. She started in the opposite direction, and they passed. Being a woman, she looked at him. He went on until he judged that the woman would be out of sight, then he turned and went back.

At the second attempt he got halfway up the stairs to Jo's flat, and stopped when he heard a woman's voice.

'Ah, but you can't get rid of me like that,' the woman cried. 'I know more than you think.'

It was not Jo's voice, unless it had changed completely

in a few years. So McCool assumed that it was Mrs. Brotherhood, telling her husband a thing or two. The husband's reply was an indistinct growl. The policeman moved further up the stairs, then turned and fled in silent haste as he heard a door open again. This time it was Jo's door, and the person who had opened it must have been standing there holding it open, ready to depart. As the inspector tiptoed through the outer doorway he heard Raymond Brotherhood say: 'We'd better discuss your ridiculous behaviour in private.'

McCool ran to his car and slipped in beside Maffin. 'Get going,' he said. 'They'll be out in a minute.'

They drove off the street. Before they reached the main road they passed a car which they both recognized. It was standing at the kerb, facing in the same direction as Brotherhood's. The two men in it were the detective officers who were currently engaged in observing and reporting the movements of Brotherhood. McCool had forgotten all about them. They had kept out of his sight also, and still they had kept in touch with the subject of observations.

From time to time McCool had had his doubts. Surreptitious observation is an art, and some of his men had had very little practice in it. He had been compelled to accept the risk that they would be noticed by the man they were following.

'That fellow seems to be doing all right, at any rate,' he mused.

8

WEDNESDAY MORNING was bright and breezy. McCool entered Headquarters and assured himself that everything was as well as he could expect. He observed that the Sayle investigation was running smoothly, but where it was running he did not know. Brotherhood was under observation, but that little fancy of McCool's was only a small part of the investigation. The C.I.D. had been temporarily increased by putting a number of the men of the uniform branch into plain clothes. They were busy on routine inquiries, the dreary business of looking, listening and asking questions in every likely and unlikely place near the scene of the murder. There was also the task of following up the 'information' which was pouring in by letter and telephone, and this was work slightly less dreary but equally disappointing. There was, too, the job of circulating in the less salubrious parts of the town, seeking even the merest whisper of anything connected with Rodrick. A little better, this, since it provided excuses for visiting public houses and conversing with characters who, if not picturesque, were at least interesting.

But the main part of the case, McCool's part, was the task of trying to get information out of Johnny Rodrick. Rodrick had already had a long, hard session of interrogation on the night of Sayle's murder, and another the following day, and he had proved to be surprisingly obdurate. He still would not admit that he had had an accomplice for the Sayle break-in, and McCool, though worried and frustrated about the waste of precious time, was compelled to rely on the patient building up of fear.

He went down to the cells and saw Rodrick sitting there, with three of his four-day remand still to go. He assured him that he was still the Number One murder suspect. 'It's coming along nicely,' he said. 'We keep finding little bits of evidence.'

'Planting it, you mean,' the thief retorted bitterly.

McCool smiled cynically and said: 'You know we don't do things like that.'

'If you're finding evidence, you must be putting it there first. What sort of evidence?'

'I'd be a fool to tell you. But I'll have enough when I've finished.'

'There can't be any evidence. I never hurt anybody and I never went into that room.'

'It was you or your mate.'

'I had no mate.'

'Then it's just too bad for you. You're it. And when I charge you with murder, I'll have enough evidence.'

'A bloody wild leopard 'ud be less cruel nor you,' said Johnny miserably. 'You'd hang an innocent man and laugh about it.'

McCool stood looking down at him, perceiving that he was really worried. The greater the fear inside him, the sooner he would tell the whole truth to save his neck. McCool understood that fear. It is nerve-racking to be a guilty man in danger of conviction, and it is worse to be an innocent man accused in error, but it is worst of all to be not guilty of a major crime and to know or suspect that callous enemies are building a framework of false evidence to make sure of a conviction. McCool hoped that sooner or later the strain would be too much for Johnny.

71

'I won't get any grey hairs bothering about what you think,' he said brutally. 'I've got to look after myself, and that means I've got to clear this murder one way or another.'

He left the man then, and went upstairs for the daily interview with the Chief Constable. Then he returned to the C.I.D. and picked up Hard Times, and they drove out to Chestnut Park to see Mrs. Sayle.

A hundred yards away from the Sayle residence a car lurked in a tree-lined lane. Pettit was at the wheel. He was one of the two men who had Brotherhood under observation that morning, and probably the other one would be somewhere in the vicinity on foot. So Brotherhood was at Fairlawn. That pleased McCool. Meeting the shop manager and his new boss together would give him some idea how well they knew each other.

Brotherhood's car, a Vauxhall in good condition, was at the front door of Fairlawn. McCool put his own car beside it, and as he and Hard Times went to the door they were seen through a window by Mrs. Sayle. She opened the door herself. 'Come in,' she said. Her manner was reserved, but she did not give them the impression that they were unwelcome.

She took them into the lounge. Brotherhood rose from a chair.

'I understand you've met Mr. Brotherhood, Inspector,' Mrs. Sayle said.

'Yes, we've met,' said McCool, nodding to the man.

She said: 'Do sit down, Raymond,' and she made a vague gesture to indicate that the police might also sit.

Out of habit McCool chose a chair with its back to the window.

'How is the case going, Inspector?' Brotherhood asked. He spoke with patronizing cheerfulness. McCool under-

72

stood. Mrs. Sayle was being shown that her shop manager was, socially at least, a cut above the constabulary.

McCool grinned, and brought out an old police gag. 'I expect to have the case solved at any moment.'

'Has that man admitted it yet?' Mrs. Sayle asked.

'He has made certain statements. I can't tell you what he said.'

'Have you found the box from the safe?' Brotherhood wanted to know.

'Yes, we found it. Sayle's name was on it. Did you know?'

'No. What was in it? Or mustn't I ask?'

'You may ask. It was full of river water.'

'Nothing else?'

'No.'

'Too bad. Now we may never know just what was in it.'

McCool made no comment about that. He said: 'I take it that you are now in full charge of the shop, Mr. Brotherhood. Or should I not ask?'

'Well, I don't see how that concerns you. The business is going on as it was before. There will be no changes made without consultation.'

'With the board?'

'With Mrs. Sayle. She's all the board there is.'

Mrs. Sayle said defensively: 'Who else will run the business if Mr. Brotherhood doesn't? What did you want to see me about?'

McCool did not reply. There was a rather long silence, and then Brotherhood rose to his feet.

'No concern of mine, eh?' he said. 'Think about those matters we've been discussing, Mrs. Sayle.'

'I'll do that, Raymond,' she replied with a smile.

McCool reflected that there was no doubt about it, the fellow had a way with the women.

'I'll keep you in touch with everything,' the manager said, and then he departed.

'Now,' said Mrs. Sayle coolly. 'Perhaps you'll tell me what you want.'

McCool grinned. He also had a way with the women. 'Don't be like that, madam,' he said. 'When this business is over you may feel grateful to the police. In the meantime I hope you'll at least be patient.'

She thawed a little. 'You have your work to do,' she admitted. Then she said: 'Will you have a drink?'

'Another time I'll be delighted to have a drink in such charming company,' he said earnestly. 'Just now it's out of the question.'

'Perhaps it is a little early in the day,' she agreed.

'About the contents of the cash box which was stolen. I'm inclined to think that it was so stuffed with paper money that the thief felt that he just didn't have time to transfer it to some other sort of container. He *had* to take the box.'

'I'm not in the least concerned about that; I have discussed it with my—advisers.'

'I think I know the reason for your lack of concern.'

'Of course you do. There was a rumour that Selwyn had a lot of money in the box. It was a rumour which I hadn't heard, but I'm told that it might be well founded. If the box hadn't been stolen, and it had proved to contain a lot of money, the Inland Revenue would have been buzzing round the estate like, like . . .'

'Like buzzards,' said McCool. 'Yes, I see that. However, it is a police matter to recover the money if it can be done, though the theft of it can't be listed as a crime, yet.'

'Of course not. You have no proof that the box wasn't empty. And is that all?'

He looked at her. In daylight she was more attractive than ever. And she seemed to be honest. His research had yielded no information to her discredit. He longed to warn her not to sell the business she had inherited, or, if she did sell, to call in a really independent expert to put a price on it. But he had to remain silent. In those circumstances his unsolicited advice would have been an impertinence.

'Is there anything the police can do?' he asked. 'Is there anything worrying or annoying you?'

She smiled then. And suddenly she laughed. 'Only the police,' she said.

He smiled in return. 'I bought that one.' Then he said more seriously: 'You see, the theft of the cash box is upsetting our case. It couldn't have been stolen by the man who is under arrest.'

'It seems silly to say that there must have been two of them. That's probably the first thing you would think of.'

'Naturally. And until we find that second person we can't clear the case.'

It had been a safe assumption by McCool that Mrs. Sayle had received few compliments from the brusque Selwyn, even though he had been infatuated by her. Since he had said that she was charming she had made a new appraisal of him. And obviously it had been a favourable one.

'You'll find him, Mr. McCool. I'm sure you will,' she said. Then she added: 'I only hope you won't cost the estate too much, that's all.'

There was no more to be said. McCool and Hard Times took their leave. When they were out in the sunshine, getting into their car, the sergeant said: 'I could have used that drink you turned down.'

McCool looked at his watch. 'By the time we get into town they'll be open. But you won't be getting a drink. I will.'

'That's nice of you. Where are you heading for?'

75

'The Walnut Tree.'

'You can have it. A right toffee-nosed lot go in there.'

'It's good ale.'

'It costs too much.'

'Dearie me, I've upset the lad,' McCool murmured.

In town he drove past the Walnut Tree. Jo Tavenant's white car was in the forecourt. He stopped a little further along the street.

Hard Times knew who owned the white car. 'Your old sweetie's in there,' he commented.

McCool nodded. 'She's my target.'

The sergeant was surprised. 'Are you after taking up with her again?'

'I am not. She's involved with Brotherhood.'

'That fellah sure can get 'em.'

'He can indeed. And it takes money to run women on the side. And the more they have of their own the more they cost to take out.'

'You think Brotherhood might be hard up?'

'No. Just another possibility.'

While he talked McCool watched the people passing on the other side of the street. He saw Wally Hunter striding towards his drink-before-lunch, and let him go. Two accidental meetings in the same place within twenty-four hours would have been too much of a coincidence for him.

While he waited the inspector wondered how many of his colleagues would have taken the trouble to do what he was doing. With the same aims as himself, most of them would have strolled casually into the inn, relying on other people's lack of perception to make their visit seem to be a chance call for a drink. But not McCool. In a town like Utterham, where he was so widely known that the use of any sort of disguise was futile, he would at least make a real attempt to disguise his motives.

Then he saw his man; a dear old acquaintance. It was
Dr. Everett, who liked to gossip with bobbies, and who
had gossiped with McCool when he was a young P.C. on
the beat. McCool had not seen the old man for some considerable time.

'Take the wheel,' he said to Hard Times. 'Drive back to
Headquarters and get your lunch.'

Then he was out of the car and crossing the road, being
careful of the traffic and not apparently looking in Dr.
Everett's direction at all. The doctor perceived his approach and smiled broadly. He spread his arms wide
when McCool stepped on to the kerb, and barred his way.
'Good gracious, Inspector,' he said. 'I haven't seen you
for ages. You're a busy man these days.'

Hands were shaken. Polite inquiries were made. 'Come
and have a drink, my dear fellow,' the doctor invited. And,
not too deeply concerned: 'Are you on duty?'

'Policemen, reporters and frail ladies are always on
duty,' McCool replied. 'But actually I have an hour to
spare.'

Everett took him by the elbow. 'Come along then. This
way. You see, I know how to put the arm on a man.'

McCool had no scruples about using Everett, and in any
case he knew that the doctor would have joined in the
subterfuge with gusto had he known that there was one.
They entered the Walnut Tree. There were only five
customers in the bar. These were in one loose group, not
exactly together but all able to hear the general conversation. Mrs. Dennis the landlady was in the middle of the
group, buying a round of drinks as she invariably did when
she condescended to mix with the bar customers. She was a
big, florid woman with a theatrical past and a manner to
match. Her hair was redder than a setter's coat, its colour
and style expensively maintained.

This lady knew Everett well, and McCool slightly. She

greeted them both with all the gush of a hostess in an Edwardian play. Then with a swift change to the voice and manner of Diamond Lil, she commanded them to name their poison.

'Thank you, my dear,' the doctor replied. 'I'm throwing your kindness in your face, but I haven't seen McCool for years, and I want him to have a drink with me.'

'The *patronne* is in the chair, and your money will not be accepted,' said Mrs. Dennis majestically. 'If you want to pay, you must wait your turn.'

'Damn it!' exclaimed the doctor with chubby petulance. 'Can't I bring a friend in here and buy him a drink?'

'Certainly, my pet. You can buy me one too. Next time round.'

All this served to establish the fact that Everett had brought McCool into the inn, but the inspector was not listening. He was meeting the cool, smiling, slightly mocking glance of Jo Tavenant.

'Hello, Jim,' she said. 'It's years, isn't it?'

'Since we actually met,' he admitted. 'I've seen you often enough. I'm the man who stands on street corners, you know.'

'A man can't do that for a few years without learning something about human nature,' the doctor interposed. 'How are you getting on with your murder case?'

'Slowly but surely, I think,' McCool replied. He was questioned further about the Sayle crime. His answers were confidential in manner but not in substance. He gave to his hearers information which was not secret, but they were satisfied that they were hearing something which was denied to the general public.

Wally Hunter and two more business types had their brief wassail and went away. Everett obviously wanted to have a long talk with McCool, but Mrs. Dennis involved him in a conversation about some mutual friend who had gone to live in Switzerland. Jo had moved away from the bar and taken a seat at a table.

'Come over here, Jim, and talk to me,' she called.

McCool obeyed. He had noticed a mirror at the end of the bar, facing the door. From habit, with no particular plan in mind, he moved a chair to sit at the table. He had his back to the door, but he could see it in the mirror.

'You've grown even more handsome, Jim,' his ex-sweetheart said. 'Maturity suits you.'

'You look extremely good yourself,' he replied. 'Very smart, very beautiful.'

She was pleased, in a guarded way. 'No hard feelings?' she asked.

He shook his head. 'That's long ago and far away.'

'Do you know what people call you?'

'Yes, I know.'

'Copper McCool. The chief of detectives. You've done well for yourself.'

He grinned. 'And you?'

She laughed. 'I suppose you think I'm a hard case.'

He did think so, but he did not want to quarrel with her. Not yet, at any rate.

'It's a hard world,' he said. 'I don't blame you for doing the best for yourself. Some people have it laid on for them. Those who haven't must do the best they can to make their own way.'

'I made mine. Perhaps I didn't always do right.'

'You can't always do right, you can only do as right as you can.'

'It's nice of you to be like this, Jim. Of course, I always knew you would be. There's nothing petty about you.'

He shrugged modestly, reflecting that she had never hesitated to flatter when she wanted something. But now he did not suspect her of flattery with a motive. No doubt she was grateful for his attitude, and probably her words were sincere.

At that moment he caught a reflection of movement in the mirror at the end of the bar. His glance shifted to it. He saw Brotherhood at the door, looking into the room. He seemed to perceive the two at the table, though McCool could not be sure whether or not he had been recognized. He stepped back, moving out of sight. He did not reappear. McCool returned his gaze to Jo, whose eyes had never left his face. To her he had merely looked abstracted for a moment.

'Were you making up your mind what to tell me?' she asked with a smile.

'I was thinking of all the girls I might have married, and didn't,' he fibbed.

'You never married?'

'No.'

'I'm glad you're not married,' she said impulsively. 'It's nice to think of a man like you being at large without a jealous wife in the background.'

'What about you?' he asked, carefully guiding the conversation the way he wanted it to go. 'It's hardly likely that a girl with your looks and personality will have been neglected. I expect you have a man in tow, somewhere.'

'Never a one,' she replied gaily. 'I *was* recently involved, I will admit. But he was married, and it's all over now.'

'And no regrets?'

'On my part, none,' she said firmly. Her smile had gone, and there was a touch of asperity in her voice.

But the asperity was not for McCool. She emptied her glass and smiled again. 'Buy me a drink, Jim,' she said with unnecessary entreaty.

'But of course!' He went to the bar, and found two drinks waiting there; a whisky for himself a gin-and-tonic for Jo.

Dr. Everett was still there with Mrs. Dennis. He gave McCool a roguish wink and whispered loudly: 'Nice work, Inspector.'

McCool returned to Jo with the drinks. Obviously she had seen the wink and heard the whisper, but he made no reference to either. 'I wouldn't think it could ever be satisfactory, an affair with a married person,' he said, as if it were a remark made to cover an awkward moment. He did not seem to expect a reply.

'You're right,' she said. Her lips curled. 'A dodging, hole-and-corner business.'

'For the married one, at any rate.'

As he had hoped, she was resentful enough to need a sympathetic ear. 'Yes,' she said. 'He tells you the tale. He and his wife aren't interested in each other. They haven't slept together for years. He's often thought about getting a divorce, and so on. It's an old story, but he puts it over very well. Then it turns out his wife is mad jealous of him, and is following him around. And she's been following him around all her married life, trying to stop his little games. At least that's what she said.'

The last remark had changed the story from supposition to narrative, but apparently Jo had not noticed. McCool pretended that he also had failed to notice.

'And when she starts laying the law down he has no more fight in him than a whipped dog,' he ventured.

'Well, not quite as bad as that. He told her he was fed up with her prying, and he was going to leave her. But that didn't shake her a bit. She said she'd been following him the night before, too, and that shook *him*. It shook me, too. I hadn't been with him the night before.'

McCool looked shocked. 'He'd been out with somebody else the night before?'

'So I gathered. Anyway, he didn't want it bringing out in front of me. He shut her up quick and took her off with him. I was relieved, I'll tell you. I'd nearly fallen for a man who was no more than a—a philanderer.'

She looked at McCool fondly, because he was unmarried and presumably not a philanderer. He wondered if gin affected her that way.

'Let's talk about something else,' she said. 'Let's talk about you. Tell me about the girls you didn't marry.'

He grinned. 'Of the girls I didn't marry, you were the most important.'

'Then tell me about me. Was I nice?'

'You were beautiful. Just as beautiful as you are now.'

'That sort of talk is going to get you a date for lunch, if you aren't careful.'

'Lunch with you is a good idea. Where would you like to go?'

'Home. It's cooking. A lovely duckling, plenty big enough for two. We'll have a bottle of wine, too. We'll make it a celebration.'

He thought he understood. This was the rebound from Brotherhood. Jo was ready to start an affair. He wondered how far it would go if he were willing. She might offer him a satisfaction which she had denied him when they were affianced. He was sure that the denial had had nothing to do with morality. It had been a matter of business. She had put a price on herself, the price being marriage, and she had sold herself to the highest bidder. Now, after her body had been bought and sold, it could perhaps be had for nothing. He did not think she had marriage in mind. Now that she was a comparatively rich woman she would not regard a police inspector as a suitable match.

From her own point of view she would be getting the toffee and the halfpenny; she had the money, and now she might be getting the man she had once been prepared to marry for his own sake. Well, McCool did not mind. He was feeling indulgent towards her. She had given him the best bit of information he had received since the Sayle job had started. And she certainly was an attractive woman.

'Get me another drink, Jim dear,' she said. 'We have just time for one more before we go.'

9

McCool made up for a squandered afternoon by working hard that evening. He had another interview with Johnny Rodrick, and succeeded in leaving him more worried than before. He kept in touch with his observers, and he caught up with his paper work. Then he spent the hour between nine and ten seeking an 'accidental' meeting with Helen Reed in the Puzzle Bar or wherever she might be. She was not to be found in any of the likely places and, he thought, she was probably at home. He decided that he would have to seek her at her home, but not that night. Ten o'clock was too late, because at ten o'clock he had other business.

If the afternoon's effort had been merely for the purpose of gaining Jo Tavenant's confidence, with a view to receiving further information about Brotherhood, it had been almost too successful. Lunch had been followed by a siesta, and McCool's virility had thrilled his ex-sweetheart. She had declared that she had been missing something for years, but was not going to miss it any more.

'I shall think about nothing else,' she had said, 'and tonight I shall be wanting you again. I know I shall. You've said you're busy. All right, I'll admit that. But you can come when you've finished work. Come at ten o'clock and I'll have supper ready for you.'

He was no more of a puritan than the average man. Jo had been holding him, using her body to influence him when she had made that demand. He had agreed to visit her that night, and actually when ten o'clock came round he was looking forward to the meeting with her.

So, at fifteen minutes past ten he left his car in a quiet street near Regency Terrace and walked along to Jo's flat. A light in her window informed him that she was at home, as promised. He entered the house and climbed the stairs. He rang the doorbell of the flat. There was no reply. He tried the door and found that it was not locked. Holding it open a little way he called out. Still there was no reply.

He entered the small, beautifully decorated hallway of the flat. The living-room door was open. He looked into the room, which that afternoon he had found to be a haven of tasteful luxury. Now, it was in disorder. The permanent cushions of the settee and chairs had been displaced and thrown on the floor, drawers had been pulled out, and their contents scattered about, pictures had been moved and left hanging awry, books from a small bookcase had been placed in piles on the floor. It seemed clear to McCool that a thief had been in the place.

Jo's bedroom door was open. He entered, and found the same sort of disorder. Jo lay on the bed, flat on her back. Her eyes were wide open, as if she still stared in terror. Marks on her throat showed the cause of her death. Her clothing was in disarray.

Rape, murder and robbery. That was what it looked like. That was the picture.

Shock and horror, and pity for poor Jo, were followed by sick anger as McCool realized the vulnerability of his own position. Somebody had made a fool of him. He felt sure of that. This crime had been planned, and somebody, somewhere, was laughing at him.

Well, Jo was dead. McCool thought of himself. He had left Jo at half past four. He had walked into the C.I.D. at a quarter to five, and from then until nine o'clock he had been almost constantly in touch with people. From nine until ten he had been pub-crawling in search of Mrs. Reed, and he had been known by the licensee of every bar he had entered. But if Jo had been killed within an hour of his departure from the flat he would be a suspect, and the main one. He had been seen to leave the Walnut Tree with her, and the old story of the jilting would be recalled.

He reached down and gently handled Jo's bare forearm. It was quite cold. 'Hell,' he muttered.

He looked for the telephone. He wanted the police surgeon first, the sooner the better. After that the machinery of the investigation could be set in motion.

He knew the doctor's number, and he was fortunate in one matter at any rate. Dr. Fraser was at home. 'Regency Terrace? I'll be there in three minutes,' he said.

McCool phoned Headquarters. By the time he had finished giving instructions, Fraser was coming up the stairs. He entered, gave McCool a curious glance when he saw that he was alone, and then went straight to the body.

'Jo Tavenant,' he said in some surprise. 'Well, well. Lionel Tavenant's wife. Ex-wife, I should say.'

He touched the body as McCool had done, then he produced his thermometer. 'Who found her?' he asked.

'I did. Two minutes before I phoned you.'

'You? What were you doing here?' There was nothing officious in the doctor's tone. He merely thought that McCool's presence was a curious circumstance which could be simply explained.

'I came here to see her,' the policeman said. 'She had a sort of connection with the Sayle job.'

'Is that so?' The doctor was peering at his thermometer.

'Yes. And I want you to keep it under your hat.'

'But certainly. Wouldn't dream of doing otherwise.'

'How long has she been dead?'

'Tell you better after the post mortem. Less than two hours probably. Less than three hours, for sure.'

'I can quote you on less than three hours?' McCool's voice was eager.

The doctor looked at him. 'It isn't often I get on to a job before the United States Marines,' he commented shrewdly.

'I wanted you as soon as possible. I was worried. I was here with her this afternoon, and there are past associations. But you've put me in the clear. I left her before five, and I can alibi myself right through from five till ten. That's something else confidential. About me being with her, I mean.'

'Of course. Nothing to do with me,' said Fraser. He was looking at the victim's bruised neck. 'Poor Mrs. Tavenant,' he said, but even his pity was briskly expressed. He turned to McCool and eyed him severely, and without a smile he said: 'It's a good thing my evidence will clear you. Without it you'd have had to lock yourself up and interrogate yourself.'

McCool managed a grin, then he went to the window. Outside a car had arrived, and two more were pulling in to the kerb. Doors banged. A rasping voice told somebody to mind where he was putting his big feet.

'Ah, here come the marines,' said Fraser.

'Yes.' McCool was on his way to the door. He met Hard Times there. 'Just a minute, Sergeant,' he said. 'Hold your men there until I call you.'

He returned to the bedroom. Fraser watched curiously as he considered two high-heeled shoes. They were standing together beside the bed, as if their owner had stepped out of them before lying down. McCool squatted beside the bed and looked along the carpet. He shook his head, and moved to look along the carpet from the other direction.

'She was dragged from the living-room, with her shoes on,' he said. 'One of them came off halfway across the floor. You can see where the line finishes. Come here and look. See where the light just catches the two lines. The murderer remembered to put the shoes side by side.'

'Why?'

'Don't know,' replied McCool, more cheerful now that he was actually working. He thought that it might have been an attempt by the murderer to get him a little further into the mire, by giving the impression that Jo had gone to the bed willingly.

He crawled backward into the living-room, following the two lines but not touching them. He reached a spot in front of the settee where neither himself nor the doctor had trodden that evening.

'She was standing here when he took her by the throat,' he said. He looked closely at a small black object on the carpet. Then he examined it through a strong glass which he took from his pocket. Fraser was amused.

McCool picked up a piece of black earth smaller than a split pea. He smelled it, then held it in the palm of his hand while he went to a bureau and found an envelope for it. Then, with the doctor, he returned to the body. 'The fingernails,' he said.

They inspected the pinkly varnished nails, and then Fraser wanted to look at the nape of the neck. 'That stuff under her nails might be minute scratchings of leather,' he announced. 'She was strangled from behind. Probably he turned her round so that she couldn't claw at his face. She could only claw at his gloves.'

McCool nodded. 'All right,' he called to Hard Times. 'You can get busy. Sergeant Cole! Come and look at these lines on the carpet. See if you can get a picture of them.'

.   .   .   .   .

Leaving Hard Times in charge of the flat, McCool returned to Headquarters. He started the procedure of obtaining a search warrant, and then he thought of something else. He spoke to the gaoler on the internal telephone line.

'I suppose you've heard we've got another murder job?' he said.

'Yes, sir. I did hear.'

'Have you spoken to Johnny Rodrick since you heard?'

'No. I haven't been to look at him since I came on at ten.'

'Good. I don't want you to say a word to him about this new job. There's just a chance he might think it has a connection with the Sayle business. You'd better leave clear instructions on your desk for the other gaolers. Nobody must be allowed to see Rodrick and nobody must mention this new job to him. I want him to think we have nothing else to do but build up a murder case against him. Is that clear?'

'Quite clear, sir. I didn't know there was a connection with the Sayle job.'

'I didn't actually say there was, did I?'

'No, sir. I understand. Silence is golden.'

'That's the idea.' McCool rang off, and sat in thought. The search warrant he required was for Brotherhood's house. He considered that he had reasonable grounds for the application. The trouble at Jo's flat last night covered that. There appeared to have been rape, so the murderer was of the male sex. It could have been a crime which had no connection with the Sayle affair, but McCool did not think so. Brotherhood had had a motive, a very obvious motive, but he had been under police surveillance. The two men watching him were due to be relieved at eleven o'clock, but their reliefs were busy at Regency Terrace. McCool looked at his watch. It was nearly eleven. Very soon those two men would begin to wonder what was happening, but they would stay at their posts.

If police officers had seen Brotherhood enter and leave Jo's flat that evening, then he was a candidate for the assizes. And McCool thought that was what might have happened. If it had *not* happened like that then it looked as if Brotherhood would be in the clear.

The signed warrant arrived, and the inspector set off for White Acre. Probably Brotherhood would not yet be in bed. A man of his type was not likely to be in bed before midnight. Not with his own wife, at any rate.

At White Acre McCool left his car some distance from Brotherhood's house, then he reconnoitred in search of his men. He found one of them, a C.I.D. man called Garnett, watching the front of the house. He appreciated the difficulties of the situation. It was a bad district for observations, with small modern houses and small gardens. Garnett had selected the only possible spot which provided concealment for himself and a view of the house. He had equipped himself with an air cushion, and he was sitting hugging his knees in the middle of some low bushes which had been allowed to survive on a small triangle of land where two suburban byways joined a wider road at an awkward angle. He was perhaps a little too far away for perfect observation, but he had the advantage of looking diagonally at the house, so that he could see the whole of the front of it, and one side.

McCool joined him, and squatted beside him in the darkness. He looked at the house. The front room downstairs was brightly lit. There were some fine mesh curtains across the lower part of the window, but the heavier curtains were not drawn. Through the fine mesh he could see Brotherhood and his wife, both sitting perfectly still, both apparently reading.

'Brotherhood has been out this evening, I presume,' he said.

'No, sir,' Garnett replied. 'Not by the front door, at any rate. And his car hasn't been out.'

90

'Have you had him in sight all evening?'

'No. He's been somewhere else in the house from half past seven till half past nine. I've had him in sight the rest of the time.'

'What about the missus?'

'She hasn't been out of my sight more than ten minutes at a time. She's been dodging about a bit, like women do.'

'H'm.' McCool was disappointed, but not yet without hope. Brotherhood had been out of sight. He might have slipped out somehow.

McCool studied the house. Its garden was triangular, because it was the first one of a group of small detached houses set in a triangular plot of land. He looked at the low, trim hedges, and at the tall untended hedge of privet which was the further boundary of the garden. Presumably the care of the tall hedge was the responsibility of the next-door neighbour, since Brotherhood's hedges were so well kept.

'What about that straggly hedge?' McCool asked. 'Did you consider it as a point of observation? It's much nearer.'

'No good, sir. Big family next door. In and out all the time. They'd have me spotted in no time.'

'I see. What's behind the house?'

'Just a little back lawn where Mrs. B. hangs her washing, and a dinky little vegetable garden. There's a little side gate which comes into the road.'

'No service road?'

'There's an unmade service road which cuts through the estate, but it's no good to Brotherhood. It starts above his bit of land.'

'Right,' said McCool. 'Where is Savile?'

'He's up the road there, under those trees.'

McCool moved off in search of Savile, and found him

leaning against a tree, no longer troubling about concealment because it was so dark where he stood. He also was
looking diagonally at the house, so that he could see the
rear, and the fourth side where the lean-to garage stood.
Under the suburban street lights the back door and the
windows were clearly visible to him.

'Seen anything?' the inspector asked.

'Nothing worth reporting, sir. I saw Mrs. Brotherhood
in the kitchen once, for a few minutes. Making the supper,
I expect. Brotherhood must be an amateur carpenter. He
was upstairs from half-seven to half-nine, sawing and
hammering and planing. He must have a workroom up
there.'

'You're sure it was him?'

'Reasonable assumption, sir,' Savile replied promptly.
'The window was open, and curtains drawn on. They're
fairly thin curtains. I saw his shadow once or twice. It
looked like him. I could hear him whistling at his work.
And I don't see how there could be another man in the
house.'

'You're sure the noise was coming from Brotherhood's
house?'

'You can have my oath on it, sir.'

'Not me. Brotherhood might want it. There's been
another job, and I've given him the finest alibi he could
possibly have.'

With a word to Savile about an early relief, McCool
departed. As the front of the house came in view he saw
that there was a light upstairs. But Brotherhood was still
downstairs, perfectly still, reading: Brotherhood, or his
double, or his effigy.

A person who was a witness to words spoken in Brotherhood's presence had been conveniently eliminated, and he
could not be directly connected with the crime. There
might *not* be any connection. McCool realized that he

might be making a colossal fool of himself over Brother-hood. This was so dangerously possible that it would have been unwise to make use of the search warrant in his pocket. Nevertheless, he was now more than ever deter-mined not to relax his surveillance of the man until the Sayle case at least had been cleared.

10

WHEN he went upstairs to Thursday morning's meeting with the Chief and the superintendent McCool had a very good idea of what was going to happen. He was wrong only in the matter of time. It had already happened.

'I called Scotland Yard last night,' the Chief told him. 'They'll be here sometime this morning. There will be a conference in this office at two o'clock. I expect you to be here.'

McCool was expressionless. 'Yes, sir,' he said. 'Who is coming?'

'A Superintendent Glenn and a Detective Sergeant Lucas.'

'I'll arrange accommodation, and see that they're met.'

'Yes. I'm sorry I didn't consult you before calling in the Yard, but you were busy, and a conference wouldn't have made any difference anyway. There can be no connection between this murder and the other.'

'There *is* a sort of connection, sir.'

Sissling said: 'Nonsense.' The Chief invited an explanation. McCool told him of the connection, of Mrs. Brotherhood's visit to Jo's flat, and of his own visit.

The Chief was surprised. 'You *knew* Mrs. Tavenant, then?'

McCool admitted that he did. He told the Chief of his past association with Jo. The matter was talked over, with everybody carefully avoiding any mention of what might have happened in the flat while Jo and McCool were together.

'Well,' said the Chief when he had learned everything, or nearly everything. 'Now I am indeed thankful that I called in the Yard.'

McCool accepted that as a dismissal. He went downstairs and telephoned to arrange lodgings for the Scotland Yard men, and for a car to meet them at Airechester airport. When he had done that he received a call.

It was Dr. Fraser. 'No rape,' he announced. 'She's as clean as a whistle.'

McCool was surprised. 'You're quite sure?'

'As sure as I could be. There's nothing at all. She's had a bath since the last time she had anything to do with a man.'

'Is there no sign of an attempt?'

'Nothing except the disordered clothes, which you saw. That could have been done with the intention to deceive.'

'So the murderer could have been a woman?'

'Yes. A strong woman with fairly big hands.'

'Thanks,' said McCool. He sat looking at the receiver after he had replaced it. Both Mrs. Brotherhood and her sister were strong, big-boned women. The sister had not been under surveillance. Could she possibly . . . ? He shook his head. He was ready to consider anything as a theory, but that one was too implausible.

And yet, who but a woman could have set the scene to make the police believe that the crime was committed by one of the opposite sex? Well, a man *might* do it. It would be an act of superlative cunning, committed with the expectation that the police would discover that there had been no rape, and assume that it was a woman who had tried to deceive them. Again McCool shook his head. Were there murderers as subtle as that? He had never heard of one.

'That's one for the Yard to figure out,' he decided, and he went down to the cells for a talk with Johnny Rodrick.

'And how are we this morning?' he asked breezily.

Rodrick's black eye was in full bloom. 'I'm as browned-off as you'd expect me to be,' he growled.

McCool gave him a cigarette, and a light. 'I'll soon have news for you,' he said. 'There's an expert on his way from Scotland Yard.'

'What's he expert on?'

'Latent fingerprints. He can find fellows' dabs in places you wouldn't believe. He'll give Sayle's office and the safe a real going over.'

'He won't find my dabs in there.'

'Ah, that's just it. He will.'

Rodrick's face was a picture of outrage. 'It's a bloody rotten frame-up!'

McCool was bland. 'Told you, didn't I? *Somebody* has got to be topped. Either you or your mate. If I can't have your mate I'll have you.'

'My mate couldn't have done it,' the prisoner retorted, and then his mouth dropped open in dismay.

'So now you admit you weren't alone,' said McCool quietly, concealing his jubilation. 'Well, it won't do you any good unless we can get hold of him quickly and find some evidence. Who was it?'

'I said my mate couldn't have done it, because I didn't have a mate.'

'Well, it's all the same to me. But don't you realize, you idiot, that your life is at stake?'

'I didn't have a mate.'

'Come off it. Who was it?'

'Nobody. I keep telling you. Nobody.'

McCool appeared to lose patience. 'I've been trying to give you a chance, but I'm beginning to see I'm wasting my time. You had a china on the job, all right, but you daren't give his name because he knows you killed Selwyn Sayle. He saw you do it. If you shop him, he'll shop you. That's what it amounts to, I think. Well, I can send you to the scaffold without his evidence. And from now on that's what I'm going to concentrate on doing.'

He opened the door of the cell, and paused to utter a few parting words. 'It's a locked door for you for all the little time you've got to live,' he said, and then he went out. He slammed the iron door and turned the key.

As he walked down the cell corridor he reflected that another day would be all he needed to open up Johnny Rodrick. The little thief really believed that McCool was manufacturing evidence, and naturally he supposed that there would be enough of it to make conviction certain. His fear was getting him down. Already the crack was showing, and soon the information would be oozing from it.

At five minutes to two, the Scotland Yard men walked into the C.I.D. and introduced themselves. They had had a good lunch at the little inn where McCool had arranged for them to stay, and they thanked him for sending them to such a comfortable place.

Both were tall men. Glenn was burly and high-coloured; one of those shrewd, genial Scotsmen. Lucas was pale and bony, with a thin, sensitive face. He sounded like a Cockney. McCool judged them to be a formidable pair of man-hunters.

He showed them such evidence as he had. 'They're both comic jobs,' he said, 'but I think the second one is the worst. The suspect has an alibi.'

'Perhaps we can break it,' said Glenn easily.

'I hope you can. I provided it myself.'

Glenn looked surprised. McCool said: 'You'll get the whole story upstairs. Let's go.'

When they were all seated in the Chief's office, that gentleman talked pleasantly for a minute or two about mutual acquaintances in the Metropolitan Police, and then he said: 'We have a difficulty. I called you in on a murder which happened last night. But we also have an uncleared murder which happened three days ago. My man McCool is handling that, so he cannot put himself completely at your disposal.'

Glenn smiled. 'Don't you want the Yard to investigate both murders?'

'But of course, if that can be done. But you know the ruling about expenses better than I do.'

'I don't think anybody will quibble about that,' Glenn replied in his genial way. 'Since we're here. we'll do what we can. In any case, Mr. McCool gave me the impression that the two crimes were connected.'

'That is a matter of opinion,' the Chief replied. 'McCool, tell these officers everything you know about both jobs.'

McCool obeyed, and was heard in silence. Even Sissling did not interrupt. Both Glenn and Lucas made occasional notes.

'So,' said the Chief, when McCool had finished. 'What is your opinion now, Mr. Glenn?'

'It seems to me that the Sayle job will clear itself when you find the man Rodrick's accomplice,' the Yard man replied without hesitation. 'With all due respect to Mr. McCool's intuitive feelings, there doesn't seem to be any real evidence against this fellow Brotherhood. At this moment there isn't enough evidence to warrant a search of his house. Nobody saw him anywhere near the shop at the time of the murder, and he has no apparent motive. He also has his wife's backing when he says he was at home at the time. In view of what Mrs. Tavenant told McCool about that, they're both lying. He was out somewhere, perhaps with a woman, and she was spying on him. Naturally neither of them will admit that to the police.'

'My opinion exactly,' said Sissling.

Glenn nodded.

'It's what I've been saying all the time,' Sissling went on.

The Yard man did not seem to be too pleased by the second remark, but he continued without comment upon it: 'Both Brotherhood and his wife seem to be out of the Tavenant job, too, though they'll have to be interrogated in view of the association with Mrs. Tavenant. I'll have to know exactly what happened the night before the murder. But their alibi for the murder itself seems to be pretty good, the house under observation and both of them seen or heard from time to time. So,' Glenn smiled disarmingly at McCool, 'I'll have to look elsewhere for my suspect. I understand Mrs. Tavenant had a husband. There's been no mention of an interview with him.'

'I thought I'd better leave him to you,' said McCool.

'He should have been seen last night,' Sissling interposed.

'He was estranged from his wife, and I never considered him as a suspect,' McCool retorted bluntly.

'He's a man of considerable influence and social standing,' the Chief said. 'It will be better for the Yard to interview him.'

Glenn inclined his head in agreement, and continued: 'I shall want a list of all your sex criminals, all your sneak-in men, and all other likely characters. Has a list of Mrs. Tavenant's friends been compiled?'

'Sergeant Broadhead is doing that,' said McCool. 'Also, men are conducting the usual inquiries near the scene of the murder.'

'Which I had better examine forthwith,' said Glenn.

'We've got one fragment of earth and one psychological twist with regard to the fake rape. We must have more.'

He looked politely at the Chief, inviting dismissal. McCool said: 'Just one moment, sir. Do I understand that I am still in charge of the Sayle murder?'

'It would appear so,' the Chief replied. 'It seems to be merely a matter of finding Rodrick's accomplice. Do you require assistance in questioning him about that? Mr. Glenn might be willing to help you.'

'No. I think he's at cracking point. Can I have one sergeant and eight of my own men for the proper handling of the Sayle case?'

The Chief frowned, and Sissling muttered something. Glenn looked amused, and Lucas, the underling there, was completely impassive.

'What do you want nine men for?' Sissling demanded.

'I'm not satisfied about Brotherhood,' McCool replied. 'I've given you my reasons, I can't say more. But I'm sufficiently interested in the man to risk making a fool of myself.'

The Chief sat in thought, and the others waited. Then he said: 'The Tavenant case will strain the resources of this force. We cannot really spare *any* men.' He turned to Glenn. 'I've known McCool a long time and he's done a lot of good work. I'm going to let him have a sergeant and four men. Superintendent Sissling, you had better name the men.'

'Very well, sir. Sergeant Viollett. Then Maffin and Savile. Three good men. And, er, let's see. Rannard and Pettit.'

Pettit was the one man in the C.I.D. McCool did not want, but he made no comment about that. He said: 'I'd like to make use of a few Special Constables whom I know personally. Simply as observers.'

'That's a good idea,' said the Chief. 'They'll probably be

glad to help you. All right then. Mr. Glenn, Detective Sergeant Broadhead will be your chief assistant from this force.'

'So be it,' said Glenn, and he nodded and smiled at McCool.

11

FROM his own office McCool telephoned the Commandant of the Special Constabulary and received his co-operation in the matter of drafting some of his men to plain-clothes duty. That afternoon and evening he secured the services of eight amateur policemen, middle-aged but keen and intelligent, and as trustworthy as regulars. They would be able to relieve McCool's five men between 6 p.m. and midnight, and he made arrangements for them to do so. Most of them had their own cars, which they were prepared to use. Without exception they were delighted to help McCool, and to be engaged in police work which was somewhat different from traffic duty at football matches.

So, at seven o'clock, with all settled and Hard Times left in charge, McCool headed for the Puzzle Bar. As he entered, many feminine glances swung towards his tall figure. He had been in the place before, but never at that time of day. 'Boy,' he mused as he made his way to the bar. 'This is a real nanny-hole, and no mistake.'

At the bar he was immediately joined by Milford Pate, the licensee of the place. Pate was a fat man, a born raconteur very popular with his customers in spite of the fact that he had the heart of a lickspittle and the soul of a pimp.

'No trouble I hope, Inspector?' he queried.

'Plenty,' said McCool. 'But not for anyone in this place, as far as I know.'

'Thank God for that. I've got a good class of customer here. Wouldn't like any incidents.'

McCool looked round at the girls of all ages, and the boys who were, in some cases, buying drinks for them.

'Nicest little bar in this town,' Pate went on. 'No Teddy Boys here. I won't have 'em. As soon as I see drainpipe trousers and sideboards, out they go.'

The inspector had to say something. 'I've never heard any complaints.'

'No complaints except brewer's blush and gout, ha ha! When you're off duty, I'd like to see you in here more often. The girls would too, I bet. They've got their gleamers on you.'

McCool smiled politely and took a drink of his light ale. 'Nice brew,' he said, when he saw Pate watching him with professional anxiety. Once more his eyes roved casually. He wondered if Mrs. Reed would be present.

Pate grinned when he noticed the glance. 'Nice girls, eh?' he said. 'I know 'em all. I know the ones who'll perform and the ones who won't.'

'I suppose the incidence of performance varies according to character and circumstance.'

'Big words, Inspector, but I'm ahead of you all the way. Character, they've all got a soft spot for somebody. Circumstances, the best of 'em have their weak moments when the most unlikely fellows can make 'em do tricks. Oh, you can't tell me. I study sex.'

In the brief silence which followed, the voice of a woman at a nearby table cut clearly through the general hubbub. McCool heard every syllable of its utterance. 'Nobody knows what anybody's doing since Selwyn Sayle was done in. That glorified lackey of his has no idea how to run a business. The place is going to the dogs.'

The speaker had been addressing another woman with whom she was sitting. Both men turned to look at her, and, being a woman, she noticed the movement. She nodded coolly to Pate, and stared boldly at McCool. He grinned at her—a friendly grin, not a leer—and turned away. He had noted that she was big, smart and handsome, in her early thirties. Her hair was a rich, dark red, her bold eyes big and brown and rather hard. He had heard that Mrs. Reed was a big redhead. If this were she, it was undoubtedly his week for meeting the hard ones.

'Those two work at Sayle's,' Pate volunteered, out of the side of his mouth. 'I fancy their feet get a bit tired. They nearly always come here straight from work, for a livener and an hour's sit down. Relaxation, as they say. But they don't waste any time. If there's a chance of getting fixed up for the evening, they're on to it.'

'Rather good-looking, the big one,' McCool commented. 'Who is she?'

'Helen Reed. Married and living in the same house as her husband, but she goes her own way. They tell me she doesn't care two farthings about him. She earns more money nor him, see?'

'She sounds like a performer.'

'Almost certainly, though I wouldn't say for sure. She's a leg-puller, and you can never be sure with one of them. But one thing I *am* sure of. She's choosey. She likes a proper man. *You'd* be all right with her.'

McCool was thinking that he ought to kick this ponce in the belly and walk out of the place. He felt degraded even talking to the fellow. This was what came of back-tracking on the trail of a man like Brotherhood. The wayside was littered with women of this sort, and the only way he could get information from them without disclosing his interest in Brotherhood was to pretend to be the kind of man who sought their company. Well, he resolved, he was damned if he was going to get into bed with this one.

He said: 'Pick your time to introduce me.'

Pate's little eyes glittered with pleasure. This was his life's work, the promotion of illicit affairs. No doubt it also gave him a feeling of power. In this case he would be hoping to acquire knowledge which would give him a limited power over an influential policeman.

He nodded, and went his rounds, and soon he stopped at Mrs. Reed's table to have a word with her. In a little while he caught McCool's glance and beckoned with his head. The inspector joined him at the table, and looked down at two smiling, upturned faces.

'Jim,' he said familiarly, 'I want you to meet two very dear friends of mine, Helen Reed and Lettice Hartley. This is Detective Inspector Jim McCool of the city police. And, let me tell you, girls, he isn't married.'

'Well, there's nobody here can make an honest man of him,' Mrs. Hartley commented. 'He's quite safe.'

Having placed a chair at the table for McCool, and got him seated, Pate chatted for a while and then went away. The two women smiled then upon McCool, two knowing smiles which held a promise of laughter. His mood changed. He suddenly realized that it might be fun talking to these two.

Mrs. Hartley was a slim, slightly haggard blonde. She looked at Mrs. Reed and said: 'The best-looking specimen we've had for some time.' Then she amended cunningly: 'At least, the best I've had.'

Mrs. Reed's smile slowly widened. 'You haven't got him yet, dear.'

The blonde woman sighed in mock despair. 'I'm handicapped,' she explained to McCool. 'I have a husband, not half a one like my friend.' She glanced at the clock above the bar. 'I can just risk another twenty minutes, all the same.'

'Her husband is jealous,' said Mrs. Reed. 'Every time she takes her pants off for somebody she takes her life in her hands.'

This astounding remark did not shock the blonde, but she pretended that it did. 'Helen!' she protested. 'The gentleman may not appreciate your peculiar sense of humour.'

'The gentleman is a policeman. He can take it.'

'I think we all need a drink after that,' said McCool. They were drinking gin, with ice and lemon. There was no waiter. He went to the bar for the drinks, and he ordered large ones to make it obvious that he was eager to provide the two women with enough liquor to make them adventurous.

When he returned to the table, they were laughing at something which had been said. 'Take her away and lock her up,' Mrs. Hartley advised.

'Drink your drink, dear, and go back to the harem,' Mrs. Reed answered.

'Now don't be so obvious, my love. The inspector has plenty of time, besides, he might not care for redheads.'

'I like all kinds,' said McCool tactfully. He was wary. This conversation seemed to him to be a parody of the talk of two nymphomaniacs. Possibly these women imagined that two utterly promiscuous females might chatter in that way. Somebody was being kidded. These two were having fun. Perhaps it was at the expense of James McCool. Perhaps, more subtly, they were laughing at Milford Pate because he was an amateur pimp.

The two thrust and parried with great enjoyment, and McCool spoke when he was called upon to do so. He laughed with real enjoyment at some of the sallies, but he was also a little embarrassed. He was not sorry when Mrs. Hartley said that she must go. She went, and he was left alone with Helen Reed, who favoured him with an enigmatic smile. He was about to make a remark which would steer the conversation into the desired channels when the woman forestalled him.

'Mr. McCool,' she began, 'are you interested in me as a woman or as a person employed at Sayle's Store?'

'As a woman,' was the prompt reply.

'A gallant lie, I think. You didn't show the slightest interest in me until I raised my voice about Sayle's.'

'It wasn't absolutely a lie. I do want to know about Sayle's. But you are also a very handsome woman. I'm assuming that you're a woman in a responsible position who might know what I want to learn.'

'And what is that?'

'Nothing specific at the moment. Shall we say, for the record, that I'm interested in personalities at Sayle's?'

'It'll go on the record, will it?'

'An unfortunate phrase. On this occasion nothing will go on the record. You can speak quite freely. You won't be quoted.'

'Is Raymond Brotherhood one of the personalities you want to talk about?'

'Brotherhood is one. Anybody you care to talk about, actually.'

'I don't want to give Raymond a chance to sack me. I could get another job, and perhaps a better one. But I have never been dismissed from a post, and I don't intend to be.'

'You won't get into any sort of trouble through what you tell me. Don't you know that the police never divulge their sources of information? In any case, what objection could Brotherhood have to your talking to me?'

'I don't know. He's a deep one.'

'Would you like to go somewhere else, away from here? How much time have you?'

She looked at him. 'My time is my own until nine o'clock to-morrow morning.'

'Good. How about having dinner with me? We'll go into the country. I've heard that the Herdsman puts on a good meal. How about it?'

'I've never been. I'd like to go. It's pricey, you know.'

'Never mind.'

'It might cost you a lot of money for no information at all.'

'Well, I repeat, you are a handsome woman, and charming company.'

'All right, let's go. It'll give Fatty Pate something to leer about. Do you mind that?'

'Not at all,' said McCool. 'I get leered about regularly.'

He emptied his glass. 'Don't hurry over yours,' he said. 'I'll make a phone call, to keep in touch.'

He made his call, and then they went out to the car. It was a roomy and efficient vehicle only a few months old. One new car was supplied to the C.I.D. every year. McCool, the boss, always took the new car for his personal use on duty. His subordinates would have thought him eccentric if he had not done so.

They drove out to the Herdsman Inn, in the middle of the rolling green country a few miles beyond the city boundary. The road was in good condition, but narrow, winding, and unfrequented. It was twilight time, fine and mild. McCool did not hurry. As the car swung round easy bends and surged up little hills Mrs. Reed was quiet, apparently enjoying the ride. He respected her mood and let her be.

When they were getting near to their destination she asked: 'What did you think of Lettice and me?'

'Obviously you were shooting a line,' he said. 'Kidding.'

'I'm afraid we were,' she admitted. 'Very bad manners, to say the least. Lettie's a good girl really. She never puts a foot wrong. Well, not often. Her husband is such a stupid idiot, she feels she has to kick over the traces once in a while.'

'And you?'

'I don't want you to think that—that anything is going

to happen this evening. I might get to like you enough. I don't know.'

McCool reflected that she was an attractive woman with social habits which would make her a target for predatory men. It would be natural for her to assume that he, an unmarried man, would want to make love to her. He could see no immediate advantage in banishing that illusion.

'I'm content to wait and see,' he said.

12

AT THE Herdsman Inn, McCool put Mrs. Reed in the bar with a drink, while he again telephoned Headquarters. Hard Times answered from the C.I.D. and assured him that there were no new developments. 'Where are you?' he asked.

'I'm out at the Herdsman if you want me. I'm going to have a meal.'

'Oh, who with? A woman?'

'Never you mind. I'm working, I can tell you that.'

'Have you got Mrs. Sayle out there?'

'No,' said McCool. 'Nor any other lady of your acquaintance. Now get that nose of yours back on the grindstone.'

He rejoined Mrs. Reed in the bar. They had drinks, and then he asked her if she were ready for dinner.

'Of course, dear,' she said. She looked around at the two dozen people in the bar. 'I like it here. I'm really beginning to enjoy myself. It makes you feel good to know you've got the best-looking man in the place. It does something for you.'

They went in to dinner. During the meal, he apologized for bringing the talk around to the subject of Sayle's Store. 'I don't mind,' she said. 'I'm having a wonderful time and I'll tell you anything you want to know.'

'Have you worked there a long time?' he asked.

'Five years.'

'You'll know Brotherhood fairly well, then?'

'You can say that. I've had meals at country pubs with him, too.'

'On expenses?'

'Not while Selwyn Sayle was alive. It'll be different now, I suppose. As long as it lasts.'

'Oh, might it not last?'

'Not as it is at present.'

'You seem to know something.'

'About Mr. Brotherhood's plans I know plenty.'

'Tell me about him. Prior to Sayle's death, would Brotherhood be in need of money?'

She smiled with pleasure. 'Oh, I say! You're after him!'

'Not necessarily. I'm just trying to find things out. I said, would he be in need of money?'

'He often was, at least when I knew him. He always had some woman on the go, you know. And I'll give him his due, he was a good spender.'

'I gather that you used to be friendly with him.'

'Very friendly. And I made the mistake of thinking it was permanent. He was going to divorce his wife, so he said. Fancy me falling for that line!'

'Pardon the impertinence, but do you still like him?'

'No. I like you, dear.'

'A serious answer, please.'

'Well, I hate the sight of him.'

'Oh, oh!'

'Don't make any mistake. I wouldn't go back to him if I had the chance, or anything like that. I don't like him at all. I look at him now and wonder what I saw in him.'

'Were you the one who broke it off?'

'I suppose so. I'm not sure. I saw him once with that Mrs. Tavenant. In her car. When I asked him about it he was very cool and superior. He thought he was moving into society, I expect. I said I wouldn't put up with that sort of thing. He said if I was going to act like a jealous wife we'd better call it a day. So I smacked his face, and that was that.'

'When you were friendly, did he tell you of his ambitions?'

'One of his main topics of conversation. He was going to conquer the world. The only trouble was, little Selwyn Sayle wouldn't let him.'

'Sayle was in his way?'

'All the time. And he treated him rough. You know, rough words in front of people. He used to wish Sayle would have a stroke or a heart attack, so he'd have to stay away from the shop.'

'Did he ever say he wished Sayle was dead?'

'Not in so many words. But it was in his mind, all right. That roast beef was awfully good, dear.'

'The place is noted for it. What will you have now?'

'I don't know if I dare. The torso, you know.'

'Well, have something on this occasion.'

'All right, then. Just a teeny bit of cheese and one or two biscuits.'

The waiter came. Plates were removed and then there was the business of selecting some cheese. The waiter went away.

McCool went back to work. 'Did Brotherhood ever tell you what he would do if anything fatal happened to Sayle?'

'Yes. He said he knew how he could get backing to take over the place. Then he'd advise Mrs. Sayle to sell out. He said he knew how he could panic her into that.'

'Did you ask him *how* he was going to scare Mrs. Sayle into a quick sell-out?'

'He wouldn't tell me that. I assume he'll be working on it now, whatever it is. He'll be getting busy with his fatal charm, too.'

'He does seem to be able to fascinate women, doesn't he?'

'Yes. He must have fascinated me. Now, I can't see it at all.'

Once again plates were removed. McCool ordered coffee and brandy. Cigarettes were lighted.

'Did Brotherhood ever mention Sayle's money box?' he asked.

'Once or twice. Like all of us, he thought there must be a lot of money in it. I remember him saying once that there would be enough for a man to start his own business.'

'His own business was part of his dream, I imagine.'

'To be a boss, and a wealthy one, that was his dream. To have the running of a concern without somebody like Selwyn breathing down his neck all the time.'

'Is he capable?'

'He's clever in a way. Let's say he's a clever man who makes mistakes. He's all right on routine matters: he can add up ha'pennies and pennies. But he'll never be the business man Selwyn Sayle was if he lives to be a hundred.'

'Not hard enough?'

'Plenty hard enough. Nobody more ruthless, I'd say. But Selwyn had the knack of making money. He also had his figures in his head; stock, prices and everything. He didn't need to be looking at a list every five minutes. My goodness, the drinks have certainly loosened my tongue, haven't they? Let's see. Four gins, half of a bottle of Burgundy and a brandy. My goodness!'

'You're doing fine. Shall we have another brandy?'

'Not me, please. I don't want to ruin the evening.'

'As you wish. Did you know Sayle quite well?'

'As well as I wanted to know him. He was a little horror. He went after money like a—a ferret. And he had about as much humanity.'

'Let's get back to Brotherhood. What's he like? Temperamentally, I mean.'

113

'You *are* after him, aren't you?'

'No. But I don't want to let him swindle anybody. Is he headstrong?'

'He certainly isn't hasty, if that's what you mean. He never makes a move without thinking about it first. And yet he manages to make mistakes, as I told you. He seems to get things too involved. His mind is too sort of—what's the word? Torturous?'

'Tortuous?'

'That's it. Too tortuous.'

'Has he plenty of physical courage?'

'I have no idea. He's got plenty of cheek, I can tell you that.'

He continued to encourage her to talk, and she did not seem to weary. No doubt she knew that he would run out of questions eventually.

'He's vain too, you know,' she said. 'There was that thing about his dog.'

'Dog? Is he a man who likes dogs?'

'He liked this one, at any rate.' Mrs. Reed laughed. 'It was a mongrel he picked up somewhere as a puppy. Heaven knows how many breeds there were in it, but it had a face just like him. You can't say a man is like a dog, can you? But somehow its expressions and everything reminded me of him.'

'Some people do grow to look like their dogs, or the dogs grow to look like them. I've noticed it many a time.'

'Well, he seemed to think the world of this dog. And then he suddenly got the idea that it wasn't dignified for him to own a mongrel. He changed towards the dog just like that.'

'Perhaps he overheard some disparaging remark.'

'Perhaps so. Anyway, he had it put down, the poor thing.'

114

'And then did he buy an animal with a pedigree?'

'No, he never did. He never mentioned dogs again. Not to me.'

'H'm,' said McCool thoughtfully, and after that he asked no more questions.

It was midnight when he dropped Mrs. Reed at the end of the street where she lived. She wanted him to drive her right up to the house, saying that it did not matter what her husband thought. McCool refused.

'This isn't my car, it belongs to the firm,' he said. 'I don't want any taking of numbers.'

'Well, thanks for a wonderful time. It's so nice to go out with a man who doesn't try anything. Why didn't you? Don't you like me enough?'

McCool breathed a sigh of mock despair. 'There's a woman for you,' he said. 'No matter what you do you can't be right.'

She laughed. 'I really have started to like you. I wouldn't have minded. Will you be taking me out again?'

'That would be nice. But I honestly don't know. I certainly don't know when.'

'I suppose this couldn't go on, with a man in your position?'

'No. We couldn't make a regular habit of it.'

'But just occasionally, when we happen to meet?'

'But of course,' he replied. There was hardly anything else he could say.

'The reason you didn't try to make love to me, has it anything to do with me having had an affair with Raymond Brotherhood?'

'Certainly not,' he answered, a little too quickly perhaps.

'That's all finished, you know. Long since,' she said. And then, rather sadly: 'And so is this, I think. Before it started.' She opened the door of the car. 'You haven't even kissed me.'

115

'That's part of the other thing. It is with me, at any rate.'

'I suppose you're right. Good night, my dear.'

.   .   .   .   .

McCool drove back to Headquarters, and found the C.I.D. deserted except for a clerk. There was nothing of interest in the call book and nothing new on his desk. There was paper work to be done, but he was in no mood for doing it. He wanted solitude and silence so that he could put his brain to work, but he knew that if he sat down to meditate in his own office he would eventually fall asleep.

He went out to the car again and started off, driving at random along empty streets. That was much better. He drove automatically, and tried to put his mind into a channel of deductive thought. It was his belief in the power of pure reasoning which made him different from his fellows, and it was this attitude of the detective of fiction which men like Hard Times found so amusing. And yet the sergeant would have been the first to admit that McCool was also a first-class practical detective.

After a time he found himself going in the direction of Chestnut Park. He let the car take him there, and as he drove past the gates of Fairlawn he saw that the porch lamp was flooding the garden with light.

The time was half past twelve. 'She's up late,' he murmured. 'Somebody there, maybe.'

He stopped the car and sat gazing through the windscreen. The leave-no-stone-unturned, explore-every-avenue mentality developed by his training was at work. Mrs. Sayle, living alone, was still out of bed at half past twelve. Normal television channels had been closed for the day. She might be reading, but the chances were that she had company. If that were so, McCool wanted to know who her

116

visitor was. In order to find out, he was prepared to wait until the visitor departed, or until she went to bed.

He drove the car a short distance further and left it in a secluded spot. Walking back to Fairlawn he breathed deeply of the soft air. It was still a beautiful night, a good night for a vigil.

He stepped through the open gateway of Fairlawn and reconnoitred. The garage was still open, and the three cars in it were the Jaguar and the Facel Vega, and a black Rover saloon: the late Selwyn Sayle's Rover, presumably. So the visitor, if any, had not come in his own car.

From the garage McCool moved along the front of the house, into the area of bright light from the porch. He stopped at the big window of the lounge. There were lights inside, but the curtains were drawn. He put his ear to the glass and heard a voice. It was nothing more than a faint vocal hum. Radio? All British stations were closed down. Mrs. Sayle could have been listening to the voice of America, or any one of many European stations, but it was unlikely.

He withdrew from the area of light and found a place to stand and watch, behind a well-grown cypress near the gate. He thought about the cypress. It was probably twenty to thirty years older than the house. No expense spared. It must have cost Sayle a pretty penny to have it transplanted nearly full-grown.

Behind the dark bulk of the cypress he did not hesitate to light a cigarette, but his vigil ended before he had smoked half of it. The inner door of Fairlawn was opened, and Mrs. Sayle appeared under the porch light. She looked this way and that, though not with an air of stealth, and then she was joined by another woman. McCool was surprised. Vinnie Storr, of all people! Stone the crows!

Apparently all the talking had been done. Vinnie seemed to say no more than good night before she set off to walk down the drive. Mrs. Sayle watched her go, then she went along to the garage and closed it. She returned to the house and switched off the porch light. McCool heard the slam of the front door. He waited until he could see what he was doing, and then he edged round the gate and went to his car.

He drove slowly towards town, without lights. Very soon he descried a girl's figure passing under a street light. She was three hundred yards ahead of him, and he let her keep that distance. Probably she was going home. 'In this town at this time there's no other place she could be going,' he decided.

He turned left at a crossroads, put on his lights and made a detour. He was waiting in his car at a short distance from Hatters Causeway when she arrived and entered that street. She was home. No one was awaiting her, because every window in the street had been in darkness a few minutes before. He walked down the street and saw Vinnie's light. She undressed without troubling to draw the curtains. Her undies were not bad at all, McCool thought, and her figure was excellent.

The indefatigable inspector was not yet ready for bed. He still wanted to drive, and ponder. This time he went another way out of town, towards White Acre. He stopped when he could see the Brotherhood house standing silent and dark under the stars. Two observers would be wondering about the car. Soon he would drive by, and they would know who had been there.

McCool sat and stared at the place where Brotherhood was, presumably, sound asleep. Raymond, Mrs. Sayle called him. Everything was going well for Raymond. He was getting away with it. And he would assume that his swindle was going to be successful. Whether or not he would be duped and diddled in his turn was another matter, and one which did not concern McCool.

As he sat there, thinking over the day's information and events, the truth about Johnny Rodrick came to him quite suddenly. And he made a fairly accurate surmise as to how it would lead him to the successful clearance of the Sayle murder.

He laughed softly. 'You and Lord Peter Wimsey,' he murmured.

Everything about the Sayle case seemed to be clear. Except one little thing. That damned burglar alarm.

13

FRIDAY MORNING promised another dry day, but dull. And there was a thin wind which held another promise, of winter. McCool, who always put off the wearing of an overcoat as long as he could, dressed in his warmest suit, which was also one of his smartest. This morning he knew exactly where he was heading but, in a manner of speaking, he was watching the signposts. His first task was to dodge the daily conference with the Chief Constable, on a plea of urgent inquiries. The excuse was accepted absentmindedly. The Chief was more interested in the Tavenant investigation, and in Detective Superintendent Glenn's handling of it.

McCool's first inquiry was at the home of Mrs. Sayle. She was one of the signposts. He was resolved that she would confirm one of his guesses. He hoped that she would not have to do it unwillingly, but do it she would.

He was alone when he went to interview her. She appeared to be glad to see him. He wondered if that were really so, or whether she was merely encouraging him to think so. In a detached sort of way he hoped that she was not concealing antipathy. He liked her, in a detached sort of way.

Nevertheless, he took up the matter in hand almost at once. 'I don't want you to get the idea that your house is being watched,' he said, 'but a member of the force happened to see your visitor last night. He thought that the matter was worth a report and a few inquiries.'

At first she had been startled. His tone set her at ease, giving her the impression that he did not take a very serious view of the matter. She laughed lightly.

'*Is* my house being watched?' she asked.

'No. Of course not.'

'The girl who was here last night, is she being watched?'

McCool had no man to spare for the surveillance of Vinnie. 'No, she isn't being watched. What did she want?'

'Money.'

'On what pretext?'

'Oh dear. I don't want to tell you.'

'Suppose *I* tell *you*? What then?'

'I won't lie to you, but I might not answer.'

'She came to sell you some information, didn't she?'

'Yes.'

'What was the information? The name of the person who killed Mr. Sayle?'

'No.'

'Was it the name of the person who stole the cash box?'

Mrs. Sayle was silent. McCool smiled. 'You may as well tell me,' he said.

She shrugged. 'Yes I suppose so. It was ridiculous. She had been drinking. At first she wanted a thousand pounds, then five hundred, then a hundred. From me, who doesn't want the money from the box to be found. I told her I wasn't interested.'

'So?'

'Oh, she went on and on. She wanted the money for the man Rodrick's defence, she said, because he had never laid a hand on Selwyn, and he had no money and she had no money. And she said it as if it were all my fault.'

'Well, it has to be somebody's fault; it's never their own. Did you give her anything?'

121

'Yes, a few pounds. To tell you the truth, I was just a little bit afraid of her. She looked capable of anything.'

'Well, she is. And did she tell you anything?'

'No. There was nothing I wanted to know from her. I just wanted her to go. She stayed at least half an hour, you know.'

'It must have been nearly midnight when she came, then.'

'Yes. She said she'd walked.'

McCool reflected that in all probability Vinnie had had a financially unsuccessful night, until she had arrived at Fairlawn. She would have been in some pub until half past ten or so, and later she had hung about in some dive, or even in the street, until everybody had gone home. Then having failed to get a profitable man she had decided that it would be the night for approaching Mrs. Sayle.

'I'm rather surprised you let her in,' he said.

Mrs. Sayle shrugged. 'She said she had an important message. And she was a woman, not a man.'

'How much did you give her?'

'You'll think I'm a fool. I gave her five pounds. Oh dear! Do you think she'll come back for more?'

'If she does, keep your door locked and call the police.'

'That *would* make her savage. I don't know what to do.'

'Don't worry,' said McCool. 'I think she's going to be too busy to come bothering you. However, I'll tell the sergeant of this section to put down this house for special vigilance. There'll be a man in uniform strolling round the place at intervals, day and night. Will you mind that?'

'No, I'll feel a lot safer. Thank you very much, Mr. McCool.'

He smiled at her. 'I'm hoping you'll thank me for a whole lot more quite soon,' he said, and with that he made his departure.

He returned to Headquarters. On the way he was held up by traffic lights, and he stopped close behind a high furniture van. Brotherhood drove into the crossing from the left and turned in the direction of Chestnut Park. Because of the furniture van he drove past without seeing McCool.

'There he goes,' the policeman said to himself. 'And she'll tell him about Vinnie calling last night. Ah well, I'll soon have Vinnie under lock and key.'

A C.I.D. car passed, following Brotherhood at a safe distance. Its occupants were Savile and Pettit. They did not fail to see McCool. That evidence of alertness pleased him. Savile in particular was a man who did not miss much of what went on around him. The surveillance of Brotherhood was safe in his hands.

Brotherhood was about to receive a shock. Mrs. Sayle was rather worried about the money from the stolen cash box, and she was sure to tell her manager about the girl who claimed that she knew who had stolen it. Hearing the story, he would seem to be sceptical and amused, but in his heart there would be panic. At the first opportunity he would make a move of some sort. It would be observed. And in any case, McCool would probably have moved first.

It was seldom that the inspector was compelled to handle an investigation in this manner, because most crimes were what Hard Times would have called 'straight up-and-down' jobs. Only one crime in fifty was tricky, and only one in a thousand was by its nature capable of producing that sense of strangeness or incongruity which could set his imagination to work. An expensive hat lying on a counter in artificial moonlight had done that. The hat, so easily explained, and an unanswered question about a burglar alarm, had evoked the mood which had made him look further than the obvious.

The urge to look further and dig deeper, with a paucity of

facts to give him direction, had compelled him to resort to
the study of the characters of the people involved. He had
had to observe, and use up valuable time in what might
have seemed to be trivial inquiry. Well, every one of his
subjects had acted completely in character, and by their
actions they had given him a little evidence.

He reviewed the evidence. There was a pitifully small
amount. He needed more, much more. And by the time he
reached Headquarters he had worked out the method by
which he would get it.

As he walked along the cell corridor, with the front office's
set of keys dangling from his hand, he reflected that the case
would be a classic. And it would be Chief Inspector
McCool's. In that he admitted having had remarkably
good luck. Not many police chiefs would have allowed a
D.C.I. to follow his own guesses in the presence of a superintendent from Scotland Yard.

.   .   .   .   .

Gently swinging the keys, McCool stood looking down at
Johnny Rodrick as he sat on his wooden cot.

'Well, and how are we to-day?' he asked genially.

Rodrick eyed the keys with apprehension. 'Bloody fed up,
as usual,' he answered morosely. 'This place is worse nor the
nick. Are you going to start the rough stuff now?'

McCool looked down at the keys in surprise. 'These?
I wouldn't need to belt you with these.' He dropped
the heavy bundle into his pocket. 'No. No rough stuff,
Johnny. No more questions, either. I know all you can tell
me.'

'You won't con me that way.'

McCool shook his head in reproach. 'I'm surprised at
you. I thought you called yourself a screwsman. Taking a
woman on the job!'

124

'Well, I didn't shop her, did I? *I* never let her down.'

So, eventually, it was as easy as that.

'No, you didn't shop her,' McCool said. 'She shopped herself.'

'You didn't crack her, I'll lay odds on that.'

'No, she tried to box clever, and gave the game away. You've been a fool, Johnny. You could have been out on bail.'

'I stuck to my guns. I never let nobody down. There was no good in it anyway. She couldn't get me off the hook. You said it was me or my mate did the murder. Well, what do you say now?'

McCool considered his reply. While he was doing so the prisoner said: 'You're not trying to tell me *she* did the murder?'

The policeman shook his head. Then he said: 'You're in on a charge of breaking and entering. That's all you need worry about if you'll be level with me. There's no need now for you to hold anything back.'

It was Rodrick's turn to ponder. 'Have you been kidding me all this time about the murder?'

McCool nodded slowly. 'All I wanted from you was the name of your mate. Now I've got it.'

'So what more do you want? You know it all.'

'I want a statement.'

'What do I get for it?'

'You get the satisfaction of signing it.'

'And that'd bring Vinnie right into the job.'

'She's in it already.'

'I dunno. Suppose I don't sign.'

'I'd be very disappointed in you. I'd say to myself: "There's a man I tried to be honest with, and he let me down." I think I'd have an active dislike for you, Johnny. I'm afraid I might dislike you for a long, long time.'

Rodrick's eyes were fixed on the grey concrete of the cell

floor, but he was really looking along the years, at an end-less prospect of being disliked by Copper McCool. He could stand trial for breaking and entering, and admit all his un-detected crimes so that they could be taken into considera-tion. That would set him up straight. He could 'do his bird' and come out of prison and have a clear conscience, until he committed another crime. It was essential for him, while serving his sentence, not to have the fear that he would be re-arrested for some past crime as soon as he was released from prison. To know that McCool would be lying in wait for him upon his emergence would be almost as bad as having that fear. It would be worse! Every time anybody committed a larceny in Utterham, McCool would be say-ing: 'Well, let's turn up Johnny Rodrick for a start. We'll see what *he's* been doing with himself.' The aforesaid Johnny Rodrick would never dare to steal as much as a loaf of bread, and a small loaf at that. Life would not be worth living.

'All right, I'll give you your statement,' he said.

'Very well,' said McCool calmly. 'We'll go to my office. The air's a bit fresher there.'

In the inspector's office Rodrick was given a seat and a cigarette. A clerk was summoned, to take the statement in shorthand, because it was considered by the Chief Con-stable that a notebook and pencil was still as effective as a tape recorder, and a whole lot cheaper. 'All right,' McCool said to the prisoner. 'Begin at the beginning.'

'What do you call the beginning?'

'Well, I suppose you cased the job?'

'Sure. I was hard up. I hadn't a penny. Be sure to write that down, my lad. I spotted this front door of Sayle's with the latch. I always like to have a quick way out. Then I looked round the back and there was this easy door. So I thought I might do it. I'd heard there was no watchman.'

'When was this?'

'Monday afternoon. The same day as I did it. When I'd looked round I went home and mentioned it to Vinnie. I said I'd a good mind to do it, only I wanted a mate. I don't much care for going blind on a job, I like to have some eyes and ears. So Vinnie ast me if she had to go without a drink and smoke and starve to death while I was looking for a mate, and I said if she was in such a hurry as all that she could dog out for me. Ha ha! That was different. She said: "Not me! I don't want to go to gaol." I said all she had to do was give me the wire if she saw a copper, and then skedaddle. I said after we'd done it we'd buy a bottle of gin and a case of beer and have a party. I think that decided her. Anyway, we set off to do this job. I cracked the back door and in I went. Inside was a sort of storeroom, all sorts of tools, and shovels and spades. I got a shovel and showed Vinnie how to wedge the door with it, with the blade just under the lock and the other end against the leg of a big table which was absolutely loaded with stuff. The idea was if a cop came round she was to nip inside, wedge the door, come through and give the alarm, and we'd both go out the front way.'

'You left her there at the back door?'

'Aye, and she must've made a proper charley of every-thing. I just had a look round downstairs, then I went up to the top floor to see what was in the offices. The offices was locked, and I was just wondering which door to bust when I heard the alarm go, and I went belting down the stairs, and straight into the arms of the bobby, P.C. Berry. That's my statement. All of it.'

'What was this alarm? I didn't ask Vinnie about it.'

Rodrick grinned. 'That foxed you, didn't it? It was Vinnie's old alarm clock, with a bloody big bell on the top. The clock doesn't go, but the alarm works. The idea was, to tip me off without the copper getting suspicious. If she'd whistled or called out, a copper outside would've known in a minute there was somebody in. But when Vinnie turned the alarm finger and made it ring, then stopped it after a second or two, a copper outside 'ud just think it was a 'lectric fault or summat like that. He wouldn't bother at all till he found the busted door, and by that time he'd be too late. We'd be away.'

McCool grinned also. So that was the explanation of the so-called burglar alarm. 'Very good,' he conceded. 'That's a new one to me.'

He reflected that Vinnie must have lost her head, but not completely. When a policeman had appeared in the yard, examining property, she had gone into Sayle's but had neglected to secure the door. She had sounded the alarm and then what had she done?

'Something else I didn't ask Vinnie,' said McCool, still fostering the illusion that the girl had been trapped into making admissions. 'Had you already shown her the get-away door with the latch lock?'

'No. I hadn't bothered. The idea was we should go out together if we had to go the front way. 'Course, she might've found it herself, and scarpered before I got down the stairs. Did she say which way she got out?'

'I haven't asked her yet, but I will,' McCool replied. He was moderately certain that Vinnie had not had the time to find that latched door. P.C. Berry had been actually entering the premises when she had sounded the alarm. He had walked straight into the place, and Vinnie could not have gone out by that door *and* slammed it behind her hard enough to engage the latch, without Berry hearing it and knowing exactly what it was. So, Vinnie had been hiding somewhere in Sayle's when Rodrick was arrested and taken away. That was as McCool had supposed. Everything was working out nicely.

'Type it and let him read it before he signs,' he said to the clerk. 'Three carbons, please.'

He rang for the gaoler, and Rodrick was taken back to his cell. He was no longer of any importance. It was his statement which was important.

McCool went out into the main C.I.D. office. Hard Times, unerringly aware that Rodrick had made a statement, was waiting there. He was not idling, but catching up with his paper work.

'Come on,' said McCool as he passed, and Hard Times opened his desk drawer, slid his unfinished papers into it, closed it and locked it all in one smooth motion. He was at the inspector's heels before he reached the corridor.

'What now?' he asked, when they were getting into McCool's car.

'Vinnie Storr. She was Johnny's mate on the Sayle job. He's just given me a statement.'

Hard Times whistled softly, and thereafter he was silent as he pondered the new development.

They arrived at No. 11 Hatters Causeway. The door of a ground-floor room was open, and a small child was sitting on the hearthrug, gnawing a raw carrot. The two policemen moved on to the other ground-floor room, and that door also was open. Inside the room two women were sitting at a table, sharing a jug of ale. The uncarpeted wooden stairs started beside the back door, which was closed but, McCool noticed, not locked. Eager now, he went up the stairs two at a time, but when he arrived at the first landing he stopped. A swift change in the quality of the daylight there made him aware of movement; movement which he had not heard. It was not exactly a shadow which he had seen, but *something* had moved. Since there was not a soul in sight, obviously the cause of the quick flicker of noiseless activity was now round the corner on the further flight of stairs. Some person or creature had flitted away at the sound of the policemen's approach, and was now climbing stealthily to the next floor.

McCool went to Vinnie's door, and tried it gently but firmly. It was locked. 'You wait here,' he said to Hard Times. He went to the further stairs and climbed them quietly, two at a time. On the next landing, which was the topmost one, he found Raymond Brotherhood. The man was pale, and very much out of countenance.

'What are you doing here?' McCool demanded.

Brotherhood took a deep breath. He actually and visibly pulled himself together. 'I might ask you the same,' he said coolly.

'I came here as a police officer, on police duty. To see somebody.'

'If that's the case I must be in the wrong house. Anybody you want to see, I don't want to see. I'll be on my way.'

He made as if to pass McCool, but the inspector blocked the way. 'Who did you come to see?' he wanted to know.

'That is none of your business.'

'It could be, if you are on these premises without invitation.'

'What do you mean?'

The answer was cool and deliberate. 'I mean that you could have entered for the purpose of committing a felony.'

Masks were off. Hatred glared in Brotherhood's eyes, and it was met with a look of cold contempt.

'So,' McCool went on, 'did you come to see Virginia Storr?'

'Are you an inspector of morals?'

'Are you trying to tell me that your purpose in coming here was immoral and not felonious?'

'Since there is nothing here worth stealing, and I am not a thief, how can my purpose be felonious?'

'There are other felonies besides theft.'

Brotherhood did not rise to that one. It could have been that he was afraid to hear a certain word.

'I came here to see a girl, though I don't know which of these rooms she inhabits,' he said. 'I am as other men, I sometimes take time out for a bit of fun. But if this is a place where the police are in and out every five minutes, it isn't the place for me. Let me pass, please.'

'Did you come to see Vinnie Storr?'

'I refuse to bring the woman's name into it, for her sake and my own.'

McCool smiled at that. He allowed Brotherhood to pass, and followed him down one flight of stairs.

Hard Times was at Vinnie's door. When he saw Brotherhood, for once in his life his face showed what he was feeling: absolute surprise. 'Let him go,' said McCool, and the sergeant stood aside.

Brotherhood slipped by, and then he turned. 'If my wife gets to know about this,' he said, 'I'll complain to the Chief, whom I know very well. A man has a right to his own private life, without being badgered by policemen.'

Suddenly McCool was angry. 'If you're going, go,' he said with menacing softness.

Brotherhood had taken a breath with the intention of making some additional remark. He changed his mind, and went away down the stairs.

'What's he want?' Hard Times demanded, when the man had gone.

'Figure it out for yourself.'

'Where's his tail?'

'It looks as if he's shaken it. That means he knows he's being watched. Very interesting. How long has he known it, I wonder? You'd better get after him and see where he goes.'

Hard Times departed. McCool turned to Vinnie's door

and squatted to put his ear to the keyhole. He heard a contralto snore.

'Lazy little bitch,' he muttered. He stood up, tried the door again, then hammered on it with the base of his fist.

A sleepy feminine voice, with a slurred utterance, told him in obscene terms that he had better go away.

He hammered again. 'This is the police. Open the door or I'll kick it in.'

'Wair'ra'minnit,' came the reply, in the recognizable voice of Vinnie Storr. McCool waited, then the key was turned and the door was opened. Vinnie faced him, in the underclothes he had seen last night. Now she was fully awake and, after a long sleep, ready to pretend that she could welcome a policeman's visit because she had nothing on her conscience. He remembered that she could have been in fear of arrest at the beginning of a previous interview, but she had not showed it.

'Ah,' she said with her vixen's grin. 'You're on your own. I told you you'd be round for a bit of that there. Come on in.'

She stood aside, dancing on bare toes so that her breasts jiggled. He did not move. 'Get some clothes on,' he said.

Still grinning, she turned away and walked with a provocative swing to the bed. From the bedrail she took a dress. She pulled it over her head, and slipped her feet into some shoes. 'Now, you want to undress me?' she asked archly.

Unsmiling, he entered the room. 'At least you had the sense to lock your door,' he said.

'I'll lock it again,' she said brightly, and she did so.

He went to the door and opened it. 'Leave it open,' he said. 'The joke's over. We're going. Get your coat.'

Her smile faded and her eyes widened. 'Whaddyer mean?'

'I'm taking you in. Johnny coughed.'

She spat. 'That bastard! You don't want to believe what he says.'

132

'I don't usually. But this time he's telling the truth. I know everything, Vinnie.' He looked around. 'Ah, there's the alarm clock. I'll take that with me.'

'It's a lie!' she screamed. 'I wasn't there.'

'Be quiet,' he snapped. 'You're lucky to be alive. When I came to see you, you had another visitor. He was on the landing. Your door was locked. Had you any particular reason for locking it?'

'No, except I didn't want to lose the shilling or two in my purse while I was asleep. There's a lot of foxes round here, you know. Two-legged 'uns. Who was this feller?'

'A chap who had come to quieten you, I think. Or he may have come to pay you to keep quiet.'

She thought about that. She scowled as she realized that McCool's arrival might have meant the loss of money to her. He read her mind. 'You can forget about that,' he said.

'You must be crackers,' she said with scorn. 'Who'd want to do me in? Or give me money either? Unless he wanted some horizontal amusement.'

Hard Times had appeared in the doorway. He was grinning at the girl's remark. But McCool did not grin. He picked up a coat which was draped over a chair, and threw it at Vinnie, and involuntarily she caught it. Never slow at that kind of work, Hard Times stepped into the room and plucked a small beret-type hat from one of the brass knobs of the iron bedstead. He jammed the hat on her head.

'Out!' said McCool harshly.

'Get going,' said Hard Times. He grasped the girl by the shoulders, turned her, and propelled her through the doorway.

She cursed him, but he kept her moving along the landing and down the stairs, still holding her coat in her arms. McCool took the key from the inside of the door. He locked the door behind him, and followed the others.

In the car, on the way to Headquarters, Vinnie began to

weep. The two policemen scarcely noticed. Tears from a woman like Vinnie were no weapon against them.

'You were back soon,' McCool grumbled to Hard Times. 'Why didn't you do what I told you?'

'He jumped on a bus to Eastgate,' the sergeant said. 'Left me standing.'

14

AT THE police station McCool left Vinnie in the C.I.D. in
the care of Hard Times. 'Let her stew a bit,' he decided. He
looked at his watch. The time was twenty-five minutes to
twelve. In twenty-five minutes one member of the Brotherhood surveillance detail would be making a telephone or
radio contact with Headquarters. McCool wanted to take
that call personally. But, thought it was early for lunch, he
was hungry. And later there might not be time to eat.
He went along to the canteen to see if he could get a quick
meal.

At twelve o'clock, fortified with genuine police-station
steak pudding and a pot of tea, he was waiting in the little
information room. The contact was made on time, on a
police street telephone. The constable on duty in the
information room booked the contact, then silently handed
the telephone to McCool.

'The subject is in Sayle's Store and all's well,' the
inspector heard, and Pettit's was the voice.

'And where are you?' McCool asked.

'I'm in Commonside. Is that the D.C.I.?' The detective
was suddenly alert.

'Yes, it's the D.C.I. Has the subject been out?'

'Yes, sir. Pettit was slightly breathless. 'He went out at
ten minutes to eleven, by the front entrance, Savile was
around the back so I had to follow on my own. He went into
the City Market and I lost him among the stalls. I could'nt

135

find him anywhere. When I knew I'd really lost him I went back to Sayle's and waited for him. He was back by eleven-twenty-five. I thought he'd been somewhere for a cup of coffee.'

'Why didn't you say he'd been out? You never mentioned it until you were asked.'

'I was going to mention it, sir. Really I was.'

'Is that so?' McCool's tone was ironic. He put down the receiver. He did not believe that Pettit would have mentioned anything of the sort. The man should have notified Headquarters as soon as he lost sight of Brotherhood. To-morrow, or the day after, Pettit would be back in uniform. McCool knew at least a dozen better men who were waiting for a chance to enter the C.I.D.

McCool was thoughtful as he walked along the C.I.D. corridor. Pettit's trivial neglect of duty—which *could* have been serious—made him uneasy about the whole business of surveillance. Apparently Brotherhood had shaken Pettit off his tail without much difficulty, and he had not been picked up again until he had returned openly to Sayle's Store. But for the accident of being seen in the house in Hatters Causeway, the man could have been moving about unobserved for nearly half an hour, without McCool's knowledge. If he had committed a crime in that period, as he might well have done, Pettit would have given him an alibi. Having already failed to report that Brotherhood had been 'lost' for half an hour, Pettit would have remained silent to save his own job in the C.I.D. He was that sort of policeman. McCool felt sure of it.

In connection with the surveillance of Brotherhood, McCool considered the characters of two more of his men, Garnett and Savile. They had been watching the house of the late Selwyn Sayle's manager on the night that Jo Tavenant was murdered. Both of them had declared that they had had the place under constant observation. McCool had a lot of faith in both men. They were good policemen. But they were also strictly practical policemen who could be expected to take a poor view of their inspector's 'fancy' ideas about Brotherhood. Could one of them for some reason have lied about his unbroken observation assuming that it would not matter in any case? Had Brotherhood been out of his house, unobserved, at the time of Jo's death?

McCool temporarily banished that question from his mind as he entered the C.I.D. He now had to deal with Vinnie, who could be expected to behave as unpredictably as a Siamese tabby. She was sitting on a chair beside the wall of the long room, not far from Hard Times, who was getting on with his paper work. She no longer wept, but tears had made a mess of last night's ruined make-up, and McCool remembered that she had not been allowed to pick up her handbag when she was arrested. She had no handkerchief and no powder puff. As he passed her he took a clean, folded handkerchief from his breast pocket and tossed it to her. She caught it with absentminded deftness, and began to wipe her eyes.

He went to the clerk and asked for a copy of Rodrick's statement. He read it through, then returned to Vinnie and handed it to her. 'Read it,' he said.

She read slowly and carefully, her lips moving occasionally. When she reached the end she threw the statement to the floor. 'It's all lies,' she said.

'You'll pick that up in a minute,' said McCool.

'Lies, lies, lies.'

'No. There's corroboration. P.C. Berry heard your alarm clock. You were there.'

'Prove it!'

'That's the easiest thing in the world.'

'You'll have to show me.'

The inspector took his hand from his pocket and held it

open before her. In the palm lay the key to her room. She made a move to grab it, but she was not quick enough.

'I have access to all your stuff. I can search Sayle's Store again, and find something of yours.'

She stared at him. 'Just like a rotten copper,' she snapped.

He grinned. He did not care what she thought. Like her current paramour, she hated the police and was always prepared to believe the worst about them. Now, he wanted her to do that. In police work he was not strong on chivalry, and for this female he had absolutely none. To him she was not a woman, she was a cruel and unscrupulous pest. He was ready to show her that he could be twice as cruel and ten times as unscrupulous. All the lying statements and rumours she had heard about him were going to appear to come true before her eyes. She was going to see danger as she had never imagined.

'I know it all,' he said. 'You were still there in Sayle's after Johnny had been wheeled away.'

'I wasn't. I ran out of that front door before the copper came in.'

'You did not. He was just at the back door when you worked your alarm clock. You couldn't have gone out and made that door lock behind you without him hearing you. You were in there, and you were still on the premises when Selwyn Sayle arrived.'

'Rubbish. I never saw Selwyn Sayle.'

'Ah, but you did. Just a little old man. Shame on you, a big strong girl like you.'

Vinnie's eyes widened. 'What do you mean?'

'Well, it's obvious, isn't it? You watched him go into his office and you peeped in. You weren't scared of an old josser like him. You saw him open the safe and take out his cash box. So you tiptoed away and got yourself a nice little hammer, then you came back and belted him with it. Then you hopped it with the cash box. Dead easy.'

She stared up at him in utter astonishment. Her mouth was open. Her eyes were wide, and he saw horror dawning there.

'Pick up that statement,' he said.

Like a person in a dream she stooped and reached, then handed him the statement. She gulped. 'You—you can't prove none of that,' she said.

Smiling, he showed her her key. 'We can transfer a few fingerprints, too. Maybe the people at the laboratory will find some of yours on the hammer. What they call latent prints, not visible to the human eye.'

'You can't. I wore gloves,' she flashed. And then she put a hand to her mouth.

His smile widened. 'That remark will certainly be used in evidence. You gave yourself away. You heard, Sergeant?'

'I heard,' said Hard Times solemnly.

She was desperate. 'I mean, I wore gloves to go into the shop, not when I handled the hammer.'

'You didn't wear gloves when you handled the hammer?'

'No. I mean I never touched the hammer.'

'You just said you did.'

'No, you misunderstood me.'

'Well, you said it. The sergeant heard, too. It amounts to a confession.'

'Look, you can't make up evidence to hang an innocent person.'

'We have no such intention. We'll hang the right person, and we'll have enough evidence, that's all. We can't afford to let murderers slip through our fingers just because they wear gloves. Murder in the furtherance of theft, it'll be. Capital murder.'

'You can't,' she wailed. 'Oh, leave me alone a minute. Gimme a cig, will you? Lemme think.'

He gave her a cigarette and a light. She thanked him automatically. She smoked furiously, scowling in cogitation.

139

He waited. He knew what was happening. She would not have needed to think so hard if she had been prepared to tell the whole truth. She was getting ready to tell him just enough of the truth to turn his attention elsewhere. All she wanted was to get him off her neck.

She smoked her cigarette to a tiny stub, and this she dropped on to the floor. 'Well,' she began, as she absent-mindedly put her foot on the stub. 'I'll tell you what happened. I was forced into this. Last Monday I hadn't the price of a drink or a smoke, and I'd had neither all day. I felt terrible, and Johnny said if I went and chummed up with some fellow so's he'd buy me one, he'd follow me and spoil it. I knew he would, an' all. Then he got his jemmy and says: "Come on, we'll do Sayle's place and then we'll be able to have a party." I told him I wouldn't. I said if he wanted to do a job he'd better do it on his tod. He said he couldn't work without a crow. The only thing he was scared of, he said, was a copper coming along and feeling his collar without any warning. He said if I put my jeans on I could come and dog out for him, and run off if a copper came, and in the dark the copper would think it was a lad running. Well, talking about running away from a bogey put me right off it, but he talked for an hour saying there was no risk at all, and then I put my jeans on and off we went.'

'You and your alarm clock.'

'That's right. It was easy, like he said. He made a bit of noise, but he had that door open in to time at all. He showed me how to wedge the door with a shovel, just in case, and then he went in. I went to the corner of the alley to dog out. My heart was in my mouth, I'll tell you, and I hugged my clock like it was company for me. I'd been waiting happen five minutes when this bobby turned out of Commonside as if he were coming round the back of Sayle's. I was a fool. I should a-run for my life. But I went to warn Johnny. I got inside Sayle's and started to wedge the door, but Johnny had the flashlight and it wasn't so easy to do it in the dark. The shovel dropped and it was only luck it didn't make a big noise. It dropped on my foot, you see. I thought even so the bobby might have heard it, and I peeped out to see where he was. Coo! He was coming right along, trying doors and flashing his light on windows. I left the door and the shovel and went through into the shop, and my goodness it were creepy! I couldn't see Johnny nowhere, nor hear him neither, so I turned the setting finger on the alarm and let it run for a second or two, like I'd been told. Then I heard a noise at the back door, and it might have been the bobby falling over the shovel. I ran to that big front door but it wouldn't open. I couldn't see no way out so I bobbed down behind the nearest counter. I was fair paralysed, I'll tell you. And it didn't make it any better when I found I might as well a-been in a showcase, 'cos this counter had glass sides.

'Then I saw the copper standing in the doorway of the back room, and I'm sure he'd a-seen me but for Johnny coming tearing down the stairs. The cop moved to collar Johnny and they waltzed about a bit, and the cop belted Johnny once or twice, and then he took him out of a little door I hadn't noticed and I knew then that was the door Johnny had intended to go out of, only he didn't know he was going to go out of it arm-in-arm with a bogey.

'Well, just then I wouldn't a-gone out the back way for all the fur coats in Bond Street, the place was that creepy. I were petrified. When I did stand up to go out the front way my legs 'ud hardly hold me. I were just going round the counter when I saw a chap at the door, so I bobbed down again. The man at the door opened it with a key and came in, and shut it behind him. He didn't turn any lights on because it was easy enough to see. Like bright moonlight, it was. He put his hat on the counter near the door, nearly opposite my counter, and then he took off his raincoat and threw that on the counter. Then he went off on a little passage behind some high shelves and in a bit I heard him switch a light on, and I could see there was a light on round the back there. I was thinking I'd been lucky so far and I'd better get out while I had the chance, but when I looked there was *another* chap at the door, looking in through the glass. And in a bit he came in, very quiet like.

'I were in a blue funk. I thought this bloke was sure to spot me. But I kept absolutely still and he never even looked my way. He stood looking at the hat and coat, and then he went behind the counter and reached up for something on the top of a showcase. Then he picked up the coat and went off towards the light. I didn't hear him go, I only heard some sort of thumps and grunts coming from where the light was. I knew what that was, and I think I must a-fainted or summat. Next thing I know this chap were coming back with a flattish box under his arm, and I said to meself: "Keep still, Vinnie, or you're the late Miss Storr." I did keep still an' all, except I was shaking like a Scotchman paying a debt.

'He went to the door and stood there watching the street, waiting his chance to dodge out, happen. He kept turning his head and looking towards the back door, and every time he did that I nearly died. But he never saw me behind two sheets of glass and the stuff in between. I think he was nervous in case the police came in at the back again. Anyway, he let himself out very quietly, and then he stood in the doorway a second or two, and then he was away. Very quick and quiet, he was. I just laid there praying for the nerve to get up and go. When I finally did get up I went out of the back door as if all hell was on my tail. Gimme another cig.'

McCool gave her another cigarette. He did not doubt her story up to that point. It had been told in a convincing way. Not once had she hesitated. She had relived the episode with such feeling that she had turned pale, and never once had she been at a loss for the word she needed.

'The first man, was it Selwyn Sayle?' he asked.

'I never knew Selwyn Sayle. It was a little man, turned sixty, with grey hair.'

'And he let himself in with a key, you say. Then he closed the door so that it locked itself?'

'Ye—I suppose so. I never noticed.'

'So,' thought McCool, 'this is where the lies start. This is where Vinnie starts to cover up.'

'Would you know this little man again if you saw him?' he asked.

'Er, I don't know. I couldn't know that till I did see him, could I?'

The inspector returned to the matter of the door. 'You must know whether Sayle locked the door or not. He'd have to shut it with a bang.'

'Yes, he would, wouldn't he? That's just what I can't remember.'

'Are you trying to tell me that Sayle entered his shop at night, and then left the door unlocked while he went into his private office?'

'No. It's just that I didn't notice.'

'To close the door without locking it, he'd have to fasten the latch back. Did he do anything like that?'

'I don't remember. I was in such a state.'

'All right. What was the second man like?'

Vinnie gave the general description of a man who might have been Raymond Brotherhood, or Frank Sinatra, or Chiang Kai-shek.

'You can do better than that,' said McCool. 'Did he have a moustache?'

'I don't know. I couldn't see.'

'Did you know him?'

'No.'

143

'Is there anything wrong with your eyes?'

'Not as I know of.'

'Did he let himself in with a key?'

'I didn't notice.'

'Did he latch the door behind him when he went out?'

'I think he did. I'm not sure.'

McCool regarded her sternly. 'You're lying.'

'I'm not lying,' she retorted stubbornly.

McCool paced away from her. He was greatly tempted to ask her if she knew Raymond Brotherhood, but already he was looking ahead to the trial. A defence counsel would be sure to want to know who had first mentioned Brotherhood's name. Vinnie would have to be the first to mention it, without any suggestion from the police.

He returned to the girl. 'I know you recognized the man who went out of Sayle's with the box under his arm. You went to Chestnut Park last night and tried to sell his name to Mrs. Sayle. You wanted plenty, too.'

Her face froze in consternation. 'That toffee-nosed cow,' she spat. 'Did she come copper on me?'

The inspector shrugged. 'Can you blame her if she did? She's not used to hard cases like you. You scared her.'

'The soppy bitch. Like hell I scared her. She's a liar.'

'I don't think she is. You knew that man, all right.'

'The light wasn't all that good, and I was looking through two sheets of glass.'

'Come off it. I was in there later that night. I could have read a newspaper in that light.'

'Happen your eyes are better than mine.'

'Excuse me,' said McCool. He went into his own office and telephoned Mrs. Sayle. 'I want to ask you something,' he said. 'Did Mr. Brotherhood come to see you this morning, after my visit?'

'Yes, he did.'

'Did you tell him all about Vinnie Storr's little effort last night?'

'Yes, shouldn't I have done?'

'Why not? How did he take it?'

'Oh, he laughed about it. He said the girl was just trying to bluff some money out of me.'

'Ah. Thank you. See you later,' said McCool, and he rang off before Mrs. Sayle could ask him why he had made the inquiry. He returned once more to Vinnie.

'I've just been to verify something I already knew,' he told her. 'The man you saw on Monday night, in Sayle's Store, went to see Mrs. Sayle this morning, on business.'

'How do *you* know it was the same man?'

'Don't interrupt. I know who took the cash box, but you're going to remember his name without any help from me. As I was saying, he went to see Mrs. Sayle and she told him about you trying to bite her ear last night. He seemed to think it was funny, but I'll bet it shook him to the core. Somebody actually knew he was a thief and a murderer. You. So within the hour he was at your place, and I'm almost certain he went in by the back door, which means he's been there before. Anyway, I happened to meet him there when I went to bring you in. That was lucky for you. I think he went there with the intention of killing you.'

'Oh, give over.'

'No, you can't laugh it off. You saw him on Monday. He killed somebody then, and you were plenty scared. Do you suppose he'd think twice about rubbing you out, if you were a danger to him?'

Vinnie stared up thoughtfully at the policeman.

'Remember Monday night,' he urged. 'You saw him in action. You saw the way he went about it. Do you think he'd hesitate to kill you, a woman?'

The girl swallowed noisily. 'You really think he'd have killed me?'

'I do. He wouldn't pay hush money to *you*! He wouldn't trust you. He'd be on edge all the time, wondering if you were going to get too much liquor and blurt it out to some fellow. He *had* to try to kill you. You can thank your lucky stars that the sergeant and I happened to come looking for you. I guessed he'd come after you, but I nearly made a fatal error in timing.'

She stared at the floor, deep in thought.

'He knew where you lived,' McCool went on. 'He's been there before, in and out by the back door. You know him, and you can identify him.'

Still she hesitated. No doubt the anticipation of blackmail money from a murderer had been her favourite daydream since Monday night.

Then McCool played his ace. He said: 'It's two months to the sessions. If I can arrest that man to-day, it's quite likely that you'll be allowed bail to-morrow. I won't oppose it, at any rate. But if that man is still at liberty, there'll be no bail for you. It would be too dangerous for you.'

She considered her predicament.

'Two months,' said McCool.

She sighed. 'It looks as if I won't get out till he's in. Raymond Brotherhood, I mean. I saw him pick up the old man's coat and reach for a hammer, and creep round to the place where the old boy had gone. Then I saw him go out with the box.'

'You're quite sure it was Brotherhood?'

'Yes. I know him well enough. He used to visit me now and again. Till he got the idea he was too good for such as me.'

So, McCool thought, another fallen woman beside Brotherhood's trail. How on earth had the man found time to attend to his business?

He asked: 'When he followed the old man into the shop, did you see him unlock the door with a key?'

146

'Yes. It was one of a bunch. I saw him through the door, while he was picking the right key.'

'All right, Vinnie,' said McCool. 'We'll go into my office, and you can have a cigarette and a cup of coffee while we take your statement.'

15

WHEN Vinnie had been temporarily disposed of, McCool called Hard Times into his office; but sat in thought for some time before he spoke. Then he said: 'One thing is bothering me. Do I tell Superintendent Glenn about these developments, and what will happen if I do? He seems to be a decent fellow, but I don't want him overruling me when I've practically got the Sayle job cleared.'

Hard Times said nothing. Impassively though he had listened, Vinnie's statement had dumbfounded him. McCool had been right about Brotherhood *from the start.* How had he got on to that so quickly? Somebody must have tipped him off. That was the only explanation the sergeant could think of. He still firmly believed that one could tell a good detective officer by his nose: not the nose on his face, but the nose who brought him his information.

McCool went on: 'With regard to the Sayle job I don't need to tell him anything, but the evidence against Brotherhood backs up what I said about his connection with the Tavenant case. Glenn should be told that, even though Brotherhood has an alibi.'

'It's a risk,' said Hard Times. 'I happen to know that Glenn hasn't got anywhere with Lionel Tavenant, and Tavenant is his only suspect so far.'

'That is so. I want Brotherhood to be left alone for a few hours yet. He's in a panic and he might lead us to that money. But Glenn doesn't care two hoots about the money. Jo Tavenant's murder is his job, and I'm afraid he'll insist on pulling in Brotherhood and having a go at him in the grill room, alibi or no alibi.'

'The alibi is your get-out. Tell Glenn nothing. If there's any trouble later, look innocent and say you'd come round to the opinion that Brotherhood couldn't have anything to do with the Tavenant job.'

McCool grinned as he looked at Hard Times. He said: 'Do you realize you might be the next inspector if I find you something to do to-night, and the job turns out all right?'

'Sure I realize it,' the sergeant replied bluntly. 'That's why I don't want Scotland Yard telling us what to do.'

'All right, we'll keep it squat and take a chance on having trouble later,' said McCool. He thought of the clerk who was typing Vinnie's statement. 'What about Smithers?'

'He's safe. He'd sooner keep a secret than tell it. To be on the safe side, I'll have a word with him. So, what's the next item on the programme?'

'I want a statement from Mrs. Sayle.'

'I'll get that for you.'

'No, you won't. I'll get it. Then when it's dark I'm going to take Vinnie to Sayle's Store, to show me exactly where she was hiding when Brotherhood did the foul deed. I won't let her know that you're around, and while she's crouching behind the counter you'll walk in and follow Brotherhood's route, and we'll see if she can identify you.'

'And then what?'

'Then we join the dog watch out at White Acre. We'll give the Specials the choice of being in at the death or going home early. In any case, by ten o'clock to-night I want yourself, Maffin, Savile and Rannard with me, with Pettit standing by in a car. Now, go and tell Smithers to finish that statement in here, so we won't have anybody reading over his shoulder. Then go and get something to eat, and tell your wife you'll be out all night.'

By the middle of the afternoon the cold wind had cleared away the clouds, and had faded away in pursuit of them. Fairlawn basked in the mild sunshine as McCool rang the doorbell for the second time that day. The inspector was feeling rather sunny himself. The way things were going he thought that he might be able to take Saturday night off work, and possibly most of Sunday as well.

Chérie Sayle's mood matched his own. She smiled upon him. 'Bad man,' she said. 'Ringing up to ask what I'd been telling Raymond, then hanging up on me before I could find out what it was all about.'

'Sorry,' he said. 'I still can't tell you. I had to arrest Vinnie Storr. I found out that she was Johnny Rodrick's partner in the break-in at the shop.'

'Was it she who took the cash box?'

McCool shook his head. 'Neither did she kill anybody.'

'Was it Rodrick after all?'

'No. I can't tell you who it was.'

'Don't you know?'

'Yes. I know. To-morrow, you'll know as well.'

She looked at him curiously. 'It's all very odd. Why did you ask about Raymond?'

'Because I needed to know.'

'Are you thinking that he's somehow mixed up with that girl?'

Considering his answer, McCool looked at her. It occurred to him that her curiosity and concern might result in the impulse to get in touch with Brotherhood and question him. He wondered if that would affect the case at all, and he decided that it might. He would have to tell her a little, to keep her quiet.

'He is involved with the girl in a sort of way,' he said. 'What are your feelings towards him? Have you an affection arising from old acquaintance, or anything like that?'

'Good heavens, no. I've seen more of him this last day or

two than in all my life before. I call him Raymond because that's how Selwyn always referred to him, when he mentioned him at all.'

'I see. Well, I'll tell you as much as I can. I think Mr. Brotherhood has been rather a bad boy, and I want you to promise me that you won't try to get in touch with him between now and to-morrow morning. And if he comes here, or telephones you, I want you to keep the talk strictly on business matters, with no questions about girls or anything else of that sort.'

'I'll promise, on one condition.'

'What's the condition?'

'That when you're at liberty to tell me all about it, you come here and do so at the first opportunity.'

'Very well, I accept that. It'll be a pleasure. And mind you keep your promise. Now, will you give me a statement about your interview with Vinnie last night?'

'Oh dear,' she said. 'Now *I'm* mixed up in it.'

'You're barely on the fringe of it, and lucky for you.'

.   .   .   .   .

That evening, after Vinnie Storr had confidently identified Hard Times in the artificial moonlight of Sayle's Store, McCool put his search warrant in his pocket with sure knowledge that it would be put to use before he set foot in Headquarters again. At last, after he had cheated, bullied and coaxed one stupid man and a greedy and unprincipled woman into telling the truth, he could get on with the job. Between them, Johnny Rodrick and Vinnie Storr could have enabled him to settle the case almost immediately and grievous later happenings would have been avoided.

Rodrick's protracted resistance to questioning had given Sayle's murderer several days of grace during which he could think about the safe disposal of stolen money. While meditating upon the possible worth and likely whereabouts of the plunder, McCool considered the mentality of the plunderer. The word 'cuckoo' was in his mind, not in the sense that the man was not quite sane, but with regard to his habits. Johnny Rodrick was supposed to have taken the blame for his crime, and somebody other than himself would be holding the loot from it. It might be in a left-luggage office in some neighbouring town, or it might be in the form of a parcel lodged with a distant friend, or it might have been posted to some fictitious address, with clear instructions for its return in the event of non-delivery. It was even possible that Mrs. Wimpenny had it. Certainly it would not be hidden in his own house. It would be in some-one else's nest.

According to Mrs. Reed, he was a man who thought before he made a move, and even so he made mistakes. That seemed to be true. He had made two cardinal errors on the night of Sayle's murder. Assuming that he was directly or indirectly involved in the Tavenant murder, what mistakes had he made on that occasion? The only clue left by that killer was a small pellet of earth. It had been thoroughly examined in the county forensic laboratory. It was not teeming with bacteria like earth from a garden or a ploughed field. It was sour earth. The scientific opinion was that it had come from waste land. When he thought about the problem it presented, McCool felt rather sorry for Glenn. He reflected that he was not doing anything to help the Scotland Yard man, either. 'But to-morrow,' he told himself, 'when I get Brotherhood sweating under interrogation, I might be able to help a great deal.'

.   .   .   .   .

It was a fine night, dark and still, and rather cool. As he made a cautious approach to Brotherhood's house McCool saw that there was a light in the front room downstairs. The curtains were drawn. He thought of the night when the curtains had *not* been drawn. Somehow he had been bamboozled on that occasion, he felt sure.

He spoke to the Special Constable who was watching the front of the house. 'All right?' he asked.

'I think so. There's been some action, and I haven't had time to ring it in yet. Both Mr. and Mrs. Brotherhood have been out. They went in their car to Number One Laurel Avenue, in Witchwood. Brotherhood stayed a few minutes and came out without his wife. He went into town to the Walnut Tree. For a drink, I fancy. He stayed there about half an hour. We thought then he'd be going back to pick up his wife, but he came here. He just got here about five minutes ago, actually.'

'One Laurel Avenue is his wife's sister's place,' McCool replied. 'Either he's going to pick up his wife later, or she's coming home on her own, or she's staying the night with her sister. Take your choice.'

'You take it,' said the Special. 'I'd sooner have a pint.'

McCool laughed softly, and peered at his watch. 'It's just turned half past nine,' he said. 'You've time for two pints, or three if you're thirsty.'

The man was surprised. 'You mean I'm relieved?'

'You are, and so are your mates, with my most sincere thanks.'

'Ah. To-night's the night, is it?'

'Yes. Stay on if you like. But there won't be a move before three o'clock in the morning, unless Brotherhood makes it.'

'I think I'll vote for some ale, and then home to bed,' the Special decided.

So, one by one, McCool's unpaid helpers were allowed to depart, and McCool was left with his five men. Because Mrs. Brotherhood was presumably still at her sister's house, he had to divide his force. He kept Hard Times with him. Savile was sent to the back of the house and Maffin was posted at the front. Pettit was taken off his stand-by duties and sent to Witchwood with Rannard.

The long vigil began. McCool stared up at the black sky and pondered. He wanted to look round the house. If Brotherhood had a way of getting out, it might be dangerous to wait.

Leaving Hard Times for a few minutes, he went on reconnaissance. Because it was possible that Brotherhood might be looking out from a dark bedroom, he found Savile at his post under the trees. He stood beside that officer and considered the best approach to the premises.

'Have you ever seen anybody use that back gate?' he asked.

'Yes. The postman and the milkman. No squeak, no rattle. The place is well kept. The garden too. The missus seems to do the garden.'

'Brotherhood hasn't time,' McCool replied. 'He's too busy sowing his seed elsewhere.'

He moved across the road to the gate. Manipulating the latch noiselessly, he entered the garden. He looked at the small, triangular back lawn with its narrow herbaceous border. In the light of a dim, rather distant suburban street lamp it did indeed seem to be very tidy. He went to the house, and moved around it close to the wall, so that he would not be visible to someone inside a bedroom. It was the further side of the little residence which interested him, for there the outhouses stood. They consisted of a lean-to brick garage, a fairly big garden shed and a dog kennel. The last was once presumably the home of the unlucky mutt which had been said to resemble Brotherhood.

The shed was locked. The garage was open and empty, and Brotherhood's car stood on the short drive in front of it. Entering the garage McCool perceived that he had been mistaken about it. Though it was of brick, of the same quality as the house bricks, it was an afterthought. A house window which had looked out on the garden now looked into the garage. It was opaque, having the appearance of a pantry window. 'Would you credit it?' McCool breathed. The window was big enough for a man to climb through.

He moved out of the garage and studied the layout once more. With the car standing in the drive, there was no doubt that a person could slip round the edge of the garage doorway unperceived by the detective watching the front of the house. In one stride he would be behind the shed, and he would be covered until he was only a step or two away from the neglected, overgrown privet hedge which was the boundary of next-door's garden. That hedge obviously belonged to the neighbour. Mrs. Brotherhood would never allow any hedge of hers to get into that condition, and very likely she felt annoyed every time she looked at it.

McCool acted the part of a man leaving the garage unseen. Stooping, he gained the hut, and soon he was in the shadow of the hedge. He moved along it, looking for a gap. There were several, down at the bottom near the roots. He crawled through the largest, making the trees rustle as he forced his shoulders through. He managed it without making a crackle of broken twigs. He gazed across the neighbour's garden and saw another line of unkempt privet at the other side. He went to it, passing behind the neighbour's house, walking on rough grass and weeds. No gardener, this man, whoever he was.

He walked beside the further hedge until he reached the short back road which served the houses here, though it did not serve Brotherhood's corner house. Looking back, he could see the tops of the trees under which Savile stood. But he could not see Savile because of the hedge through which he had crawled. He vaulted a low wall and walked away along the service road, having proved that Brotherhood could leave his house at any time without being seen by the police. From the end of the service road he made a circuitous way back to where he had left Hard Times.

He was worried. His discovery of the way out through the garage had come a little late. Brotherhood might not have been in the house for more than five minutes after his return. He might be out somewhere. It was no use listening at the window to try to make sure of his presence. The man would not be talking to himself.

McCool and Hard Times moved along to a position from which they could clearly see Brotherhood's garage. They found cover behind a well-grown shrub in a garden, and peered through the outer foliage. The inspector explained how Brotherhood could get out by way of the garage. 'We'll have to keep it in view all the time, and I mean *all* the time,' he concluded.

They waited and watched. Brotherhood's light went out. A light appeared in the front bedroom. Brotherhood was seen to draw the curtains. Presently the bedroom light was extinguished. McCool's anxiety was allayed. His suspect was still in the house. Now, he would not get out without being seen.

One by one the lighted windows of the neighbourhood went dark, until the sparse street lights were the only illumination. Hard Times suggested that they should take turns in watching. Without moving his glance from the garage across the way, McCool turned down the suggestion. He pointed in the direction of a tiny open summer-house, without looking at it. 'Have a break if you like,' he said. 'I'm not taking my eyes off that garage.'

Somewhere a church clock struck midnight. The vigil went on. At one o'clock Hard Times muttered: 'How long yet?'

'If he hasn't made a move by three o'clock, I think we'll go and get him,' McCool replied.

The sergeant's silence somehow conveyed his feelings. It might be the biggest job of his career, but for Pete's sake he wished it would get going.

Five minutes later McCool discerned a flicker of movement near the garage. It was momentary, but exactly where he had expected it to be. He reached out and grasped Hard Times' forearm, commanding stillness. He listened. There was a faint but unmistakable rustling as Brotherhood went through a gap in his neighbour's privet hedge. 'Stay here, in case I'm mistaken,' McCool whispered, and then he moved away.

He vaulted the low garden gate and ran silently on rubber soles along the street. At the corner of the first cross street he waited, and saw a man emerge from the service road. The man looked in McCool's direction, but when he did so the inspector was not even peeping. When he did venture to take another look, the man was walking away from him.

He did not move. It was a dark corner where he stood, and the next corner was well lighted. The man passed under the light and disappeared round the corner. Still McCool did not move. Forty seconds later he discerned the obtrusion of part of a head, as the man looked back.

The head disappeared, but McCool remained still. Brotherhood—there was no doubt of his identity—seemed to be going in the direction of Witchwood, where his wife was sleeping. He might still be waiting at that corner, ready to take another peep, or he might be striding rapidly away. He was being so careful that there was a great risk in following him. McCool decided to gamble on the guess that he was going to Witchwood, and use the car to get there before him.

He went back to Hard Times. 'It's him, all right,' he said, 'and he's on his toes. Going to Mrs. Wimpenny's, I think. We'll have to get there ahead of him.'

With McCool driving as quietly as possible, they made a

wide detour to reach Witchwood without letting Brotherhood hear the car. They parked the vehicle out of sight a
good three hundred yards beyond No. 1 Laurel Avenue, and
hurried to locate Rannard and Pettit. Those two were
hidden behind a hedge within forty yards of the house they
were watching, and McCool reflected that it was a good
thing he had come along ahead of Brotherhood.

'Come on, out of it,' he urged in a whisper. 'Brotherhood
is on his way, and I'm sure he'll reconnoitre. He's being real
careful.'

They retreated a hundred yards, into the grounds of a
private nursing home. They had to climb a six-foot wall, but
the ground behind the wall had been built up to a height of
four feet. Once again there was the ubiquitous privet, a tall
hedge of it growing over the wall. They could look through
it and see Mrs. Wimpenny's house.

The house was a better subject for observation than
Brotherhood's. It was a semi-detached with a front door and
a side door. It was on the outside of a left-hand bend in the
road, and on the corner of a by-road which veered away at
the bend. Because of this only the inaccessible back of the
house was concealed from the men in the grounds of the
nursing home. They could see both doors of the house, both
gates, and the closed door of a little garage at the side. At
the back of the property there was no straggling privet, but
a solid windbreak fence five feet high, covered and sur-
mounted by a tangle of climbing roses. It was, McCool
thought, highly satisfactory. Unless he found a ladder to get
him over the climbing roses, Brotherhood could not possibly
enter Mrs. Wimpenny's house without being seen.

While the four men waited, quiet and still, in the grounds
of the nursing home, their leader considered the motives of
the man whose arrival they expected. Unless he had
abruptly changed direction, Laurel Avenue was his
objective. Between White Acre and Witchwood, and indeed

nowhere on that side of the city, was there a likely hiding place for a bundle of stolen money. There were many small, modern houses with neat, small gardens, and some larger, older houses now used as nursery schools, clinics, branch libraries, insurance offices and so forth, with grounds invariably well kept. And if the money was hidden in the countryside beyond, Brotherhood would have to pass along this road to get to it.

He must have sneaked out to pick up his plunder. McCool could not imagine that he had any other aims. Perhaps he had decided that his arrest was imminent, that the only thing for him to do was to run for his life. Or perhaps he had left his very hot parcel in the care of his sister-in-law, and had now decided that it must be moved to a safer place. Mrs. Wimpenny was involved in the business somehow, McCool felt sure.

In the utter silence of that dark garden, with not the slightest breeze to rustle in the trees, the inspector dwelt upon the contradiction of Brotherhood's alibi on the night of Jo Tavenant's murder and the recent discovery of his secret way out at White Acre. He could not reconcile the one with the other. That was one for the book, he decided. A real puzzler.

Then he was tense, scarcely breathing. By his side, squatting to peer through the sparse lower branches of the privet, excitable Detective Rannard made an eager little sound, like the whimper of a very small dog. The man they waited for had appeared, suddenly and silently, in the wide, open gateway of the private commercial school on the opposite corner.

16

McCool was thankful that he had decided to move his men some distance back from Rowena Wimpenny's house. As he had expected, Brotherhood was carefully searching the area, to assure himself that there were no policemen about. He stood in the school gateway, peering round the gatepost in the direction of his sister-in-law's house. Obviously he thought he was moving in a wide enough circle to be behind the backs of any watching detectives, and in normal circumstances he would have been.

Having taken a good look down the road, Brotherhood turned and surveyed the immediate neighbourhood. His glance swept along the privet above the wall of the nursing home, but there was no movement for him to see. He flitted across the road and into the grounds of a children's clinic, and vanished behind the building. The men behind the hedge remained still, waiting for a word from McCool.

Seven minutes later Brotherhood crossed their line of vision again, and this time he was much nearer to Laurel Avenue. McCool also decided to move nearer, so that later he would be able to say with certainty who was Mrs. Wimpenny's late-night visitor. He led his men through gardens and over walls until they were in the original position occupied by Rannard and Pettit.

Brotherhood reappeared again, crossing the road and going directly towards Mrs. Wimpenny's house. The watchers were able to note the set paleness of his face as he passed near the street light on the corner. He entered by the front gate, paused for a moment at the front door to insert a key, then went into the house. The door closed behind him.

'What now? What's his game?' Rannard demanded in a hoarse whisper of Hard Times.

'He's just called for a cup of tea,' the sergeant replied with muted vehemence. 'Shut up!'

McCool did not count the number of seconds, but not many more than a hundred elapsed before Brotherhood reappeared. He closed the front door very quietly, and the watchers could only just hear the gentle click of the latch. He stood with his back to the door for a little while, watching and listening. Then he emerged by way of the front gate and went off at a quick walk towards White Acre.

McCool was puzzled, and slightly disappointed. Brotherhood was not carrying a parcel, nor were his pockets bulging. What then was the reason for his secret visit?

The inspector made up his mind. 'All right,' he said quietly. 'Rannard can stay with me. I want to look round that place. You, Sergeant, take Pettit and see that Brotherhood goes straight home. You'll have to get your skates on. I don't think it matters much now if he sees you. Just don't lose him, that's all.'

They quitted the garden. Keenly obedient and no longer doubtful of McCool's ideas, Hard Times and Pettit hurried after Brotherhood. The other two went at a slower pace towards No. 1 Laurel Avenue. McCool led the way to the front door. It was locked, as he expected. He looked up at the bedroom windows. He went to the back of the house. The side door also was locked and every window of the place was closed. Apparently neither of the occupants liked to have their windows open. The garage was locked, and Mrs. Wimpenny's little car was inside.

Every ground-floor window of the house was effectively curtained, and McCool could see nothing of the interior.

He stood by the front door and pondered. There seemed to be no feasible reason for the visit. He wished he could see something of the inside of the house.

'Got your torch?' he asked Rannard.

'Yessir.'

'See if you can see anything through the letter box.'

The letter box was a foot from the bottom of the door, and of the common horizontal type with a spring lid, so that letters and newspapers could be dropped on to the doormat behind it. Rannard had to get down on hands and knees. He thumbed back the lid and inserted his torch. McCool could see light through the semi-opaque glass panes of the door. Rannard put his face to the letter box, to look along the beam of his torch.

'I can't see anything, much, sir,' he said. 'Just the hall carpet and the foot of the stairs. The door through to the kitchen seems to be open.'

'Ah well, never mind,' said McCool.

'Faugh!' growled Rannard. He pulled his head back from the aperture. 'Phew!'

'What is it?'

'Gas. Stinking gas. The place reeks of it.

McCool went down beside him. He sniffed. 'Gas, right enough,' he muttered. He ran round to the kitchen window, stopped, and pulled off one of his shoes. Holding the shoe as if it were a club, he smashed the window near the catch. When he had pulled the window open his nose told him that the gas was billowing out in great strength.

Rannard already had his handkerchief tied round his face, and what good that was going to do McCool did not know. The young man climbed through the window while the inspector was putting on his shoe. He opened the side door immediately, and switched on the light. McCool entered, and looked at the gas cooker. All the taps were turned on to the full. He pointed, and Rannard nodded.

Rannard turned off the taps by holding the edges of them, even though it was unlikely that they would retain identifiable fingerprints

McCool beckoned, and he and Rannard stepped outside. 'Breathe deep,' he said. 'We'll let the kitchen clear for a minute. I don't think anybody will be dead yet.'

They inhaled deeply several times, and then McCool said: 'We'll go straight upstairs now. We'll take a bedroom each. Walk in and open the windows wide. Then look for a gas fire, and, if there is one, turn it off. Right?'

'Right, sir,' said Rannard. After long hours of dreary surveillance duty, he was enjoying himself immensely.

They re-entered the house. 'Notice that the doors of these other rooms are closed,' McCool said as they went along the hallway. Upstairs there were four doors on a landing, and two of them were open. The two men separated, each going through an open doorway. McCool found himself in the front bedroom of the house. He switched on the light, and saw that there was a gas fire. It was turned on, no doubt emitting a great volume of gas. He turned it off, and then he drew back the curtains and opened the window wide.

There was a large double bed, in which Mrs. Wimpenny lay snoring gently. He shook her, and found her hard to rouse. He looked at the bedside table and saw a small box of Soneryl tablets. She must have taken more than one tablet, he thought, or else the gas had already affected her deeply. At any rate there was no time for delicacy. He threw back the bedclothes and dragged the woman from the bed, and manhandled her to the window. When her head was over the sill he called: 'Rannard!'

'Yessir?'

'If you can't wake that woman in there get her to the window!'

'Have done that. And she's awake.'

'You're lucky. Mine's out, and she weighs a ton.'

Then Mrs. Wimpenny awoke. She gagged, and was sick. 'Wasser masser?' she demanded when she could speak. McCool did not answer. He left her hanging over the sill while he got a chair for her. When she was seated he made her lean forward towards fresh air. 'Catch me dessa cold,' she complained, but she seemed to realize that she had to have air.

Rannard and Mrs. Brotherhood entered the room. 'This one wasn't so bad, sir,' the detective said. 'No gas fire.'

Nevertheless, the woman looked grey. 'How many Soneryl tablets did *you* take?' McCool asked.

She pulled her dressing-gown more closely about her, as if he had made an indecent suggestion. 'Two,' she replied. Her eyes were hostile. They moved to her sister. 'Is she ill?'

'She'll be all right,' McCool replied. 'If she has a warm dressing-gown, perhaps you could get it? And is there any brandy or whisky in the house?'

Rannard was sent downstairs, and he returned with an unopened half-bottle of Martell and two glasses. Mrs. Brotherhood found a dressing-gown and managed to get her sister's arms into the sleeves.

Whether or not brandy was the proper thing to give Mrs. Wimpenny, it appeared to revive her. She stood up unaided and pulled the dressing-gown about her. She seemed to notice the two men for the first time, and her hands went to her hair. She patted it vaguely. She had a certain likeness to her sister, but she was better-looking and more womanly in outline. Looking her best, McCool thought, she would be quite handsome.

'We'd better give the gas time to clear away downstairs,' he said. 'Could we move to your room, Mrs. Brotherhood?'

Mrs. Wimpenny made the journey with only a little help. In the other bedroom the air was clearer. McCool closed the door, but he left the window open. He remained standing in the middle of the room. Rannard leaned against the door-post. The two women sat side by side on the bed.

'I'll have another drop of that medicine, if you don't mind,' said Mrs. Wimpenny.

Rannard brought the brandy. While he was pouring a drink,ᵕ Mrs. Brotherhood reached to the bedside table for her spectacles. She put them on.

Seeing the movement, McCool realized that her face had had a naked look without the glasses. Also, he perceived now of whom Brotherhood's looks reminded him. He was like his wife.

'Would you take your glasses off for a moment, Mrs. Brotherhood?' he asked.

Behind the lenses the eyes flashed balefully. 'I will not,' she said.

He shrugged. It was of no importance, though he wondered why he had not noticed it before. It was common enough, and could be seen in almost every issue of the local paper; weddings, silver weddings, golden weddings. In one photograph out of three or four there was a marked likeness of wife to husband. Darby and Joan, Dick and Liddy. Men sometimes cherished dogs without being aware of a vague likeness to themselves, and many men had been originally attracted to their wives because they were of the same facial type as themselves. Ursula Brotherhood nowadays was gaunt, and Raymond Brotherhood was handsome, and yet the similarity of noses, mouths, chins and foreheads was striking. The young Brotherhood had been sufficiently pleased with his own appearance to marry a girl who resembled him. It was another minor aspect of his character.

Well, to work. McCool looked at the two sisters sitting side by side on the bed, and began: 'Mrs. Brotherhood, what made you sleep here tonight?'

'Because I can't sleep at home, with policemen staring at

165

the house day and night. My husband—I thought I might get some peace if I stayed here.'

'Was it your own idea?'

'I don't know. Yes, I think so.'

'Did your husband offer any objection?'

'No. He said the constant supervision was enough to get on anybody's nerves.'

McCool turned to Rowena Wimpenny. 'Didn't you mind your sister sleeping here?'

'Of course not. She can sleep here any time she likes.'

'Mrs. Brotherhood, how long have you been aware of police supervision at your house?'

'Why should I tell you that?'

'Was it yourself or your husband who first noticed it?'

'I don't know. You'd better ask him.'

'Very well, I will. Have either of you ladies any knowledge which might put him in danger?'

'Certainly not,' Ursula replied.

'Of course we haven't,' said Rowena.

McCool noted that neither of the women asked him what kind of danger he had in mind. He said bluntly: 'Well, it certainly looks as if somebody tried to murder you both. A man entered this house at twenty minutes to two. He entered by the front door and left two minutes later. After he had gone, this constable and I looked around the house. Fortunately for you he smelled gas. We had to break a window to get in. Every tap of the gas cooker was turned on full, and all doors were closed to encourage the gas to drift upstairs. Up here, all doors except your two bedroom doors were closed. Mrs. Wimpenny's gas fire was turned on full. Did either of you go to sleep with your bedroom door open?'

'Both of us did,' said Ursula.

Rowena looked at her. 'My door was closed when I went to sleep. I thought yours was, too.'

'Well, it wasn't,' came the tart rejoinder. The next words

166

were addressed to McCool. 'This man who came, did he have a key?'

'He appeared to open the door with a key.'

'Then it wasn't my husband. He doesn't have a key.'

This was it. McCool struck. 'It most certainly was your husband, and as I said, he had a key.'

Ursula looked at Rowena, and the latter lady could not meet the glance.

'How long has this been going on?' Ursula demanded with glinting eyes. She seemed to have forgotten about the two policemen.

'It hasn't been going on,' Rowena answered lamely. 'Raymond got that key years ago, when George was alive. George gave it to him for something or other. I'd forgotten he had it.'

'And does it fit the new lock you had fitted last year?' Ursula spat. 'I know you. Ever since George died you've badly wanted a man, until just recently. So *that's* why you were willing to help! My own sister!'

'I tell you it was over and done with. There never was anything anyway. Raymond asked for a key and I gave him one, but he never used it.'

'But you were living in hopes, eh?' said Ursula with great malice. 'I don't believe a word you say.'

McCool did not believe her either. In his opinion the affair had been recent enough for Rowena to be so appalled by the unexpected discovery of it that she had been unable to summon her wits and invent a plausible lie about the key.

But Rowena rallied. The fat was in the fire, and she made up her mind to let it burn. 'It was your fault for marrying a one-man choir trip,' she said. 'He's never been content with one woman at a time, or even two. If it hadn't been me it would have been somebody else, and you know it. And furthermore, we aren't doing any good talking about it in front of two detectives.'

But for the moment Ursula did not care about the detectives. 'No wonder you were as anxious as I was to stop him carrying on with—that other woman. You wanted him to come back to you.'

'Rubbish. I was helping you. But not any more. He tried to murder us both.'

'He didn't!' Ursula said passionately. But it was obvious that her vehemence was needed to convince herself as much as anyone else.

'He knew what he was doing,' Rowena said shrewdly. 'With the police watching your house he'd have got clean away with it. It would have looked like a suicide pact. He's clever. Too clever for me. I've finished.'

Ursula had no answer to that. She stared abjectly at the window. Ready to call for her attention, McCool moved to the window and leaned with his back to the sill. Instantly her eyes shifted and focused on him. He reflected that he had her attention, all right. He noticed that Rowena was watching him too, but not so anxiously. There was a hint of grim amusement in her face.

'All right,' he said. 'Let us talk about the murder of Selwyn Sayle. Shall we do our talking here, or at the police station?'

17

'I'm not keen on going to any police station. Not at this time of night,' said Rowena.

'All right,' said McCool agreeably. 'We'll talk here. I think I can close this window now.'

'Leave it open, there's still gas,' said Ursula. 'Can't we go downstairs now?'

'If you like. But before we go I'll see what there is about this window which makes you so jumpy.'

He turned to the window and pushed the rich, dark-blue velvet curtains further back. He looked at the sides of the window frame. They were unbroken slabs of wood, painted glossy white. He brought out his torch and shone its beam up under the wooden pelmet. Then, standing on a chair, he looked along the top of the pelmet. There was nothing, not even dust. Torch in hand, he leaned out of the window and examined the brickwork around it.

'H'm. There doesn't seem to be anything,' he commented, seemingly without much interest.

The two women had been watching him with fascinated attention, and when he turned away from the window Ursula's relief was too great to be entirely disguised. 'Really,' he thought, 'these two are like babes in arms compared to a little twister like Vinnie Storr.' He began to examine the curtains. He drew them across the window, and then taking one of them by the bottom hem he stepped back and held it spread out. Near the bottom, and almost on the edge nearest to the side of the window, there was a tiny metallic glitter. He turned over the corner of the curtain. Attached with a big safety pin to the reverse side was a long manilla envelope.

There was absolute silence in the room as he detached the envelope from the curtain. He saw that there was writing on it, and he read it aloud. 'To be opened in the event of my untimely death, and not before. Ursula Brotherhood.'

Ursula was on her feet. 'You don't open it!' she cried. 'It's my property. Give it to me!'

He slipped the envelope into his pocket. 'It won't be opened,' he said. 'If you wrote the contents they can't be used as evidence against your husband. But the fact that the envelope exists might be evidence of a sort. I can't run any risk of its being destroyed before a decision has been made about it.'

She glared at him. Her lip curled. 'You'll open it as soon as my back is turned.'

He was unmoved. 'You'll just have to take my word for it. Or, if you like, we'll find some wax and seal it. It didn't serve its purpose, did it? It didn't stop your husband from trying to kill you.'

'He'd have come back this morning and found us dead,' said Rowena. 'He'd have found the envelope and burned it before he called the police.'

'Naturally he would know about it,' said McCool. 'Its only purpose was to restrain him.'

Rowena sighed, and got up to help herself to some more brandy. 'It's all over, Ursula,' she said. 'Now they've got that envelope.'

'I want to know about Monday night,' McCool said to her. 'Between nine and ten, were you in Commonside?'

'Yes, we were in my car,' the woman replied. 'I don't see why I should protect a man who tried to murder me. I can testify that I saw Selwyn Sayle go into the shop, and I saw Raymond cross the road and go in a minute after. He was

170

in about five minutes, and he came out and went back to his car, which was in front of the Walnut Tree. He drove off, and I drove after him. He went down to the river at Broad Bank and stopped there. We stopped a long way off, because I thought there was something funny. He went to the river bank and I heard a splash, as if he'd thrown something in. Ursula wanted to keep on following him, but I got frightened. I had a feeling something bad had happened. I drove Ursula straight home and then came on here.'

Ursula burst into tears. 'Oh, Rona,' she cried.

'It'll have to come out, my dear. He's got it all in your handwriting in his pocket.'

McCool perceived that both women had failed to understand that Ursula's document could not be used by the prosecution as a statement of evidence. Well, he had told them plainly enough. He did not feel that he was compelled to tell them again.

He tapped the pocket which contained the envelope, and addressed Ursula. 'I am assuming that what is written here only concerns itself with the murder of Selwyn Sayle. You wouldn't try to protect yourself with an account of the preparations for the murder of Josephine Tavenant, because in that matter you would at least be an accessary before the fact.'

But the arrow at random failed to find its mark. Ursula dried her tears and looked thoughtful. Her sister stared open-mouthed at her, obviously not having had the slightest suspicion that she had been involved in the Tavenant murder.

McCool waited, trying to look as if he knew everything.

'I don't know what you're talking about,' Ursula said.

'I think you do. Mrs. Tavenant was murdered because you made a revealing statement in her presence, when you caught your husband at her flat on Tuesday night. He started to defy you, and you let him know that you'd been

171

watching him the night before. When you told him that, he got you away from there quickly. Then he began to wonder if Mrs. Tavenant had guessed the truth.'

'I don't know what you're talking about,' Ursula repeated.

For the time being, McCool gave up on that. He asked: 'Where did your husband hide the money he took from Sayle's cash box?'

'I don't know what you're talking about.'

'All right. I'm going to leave you here, and this officer will be outside the house, to make sure you are quite safe. Mrs. Wimpenny, I want you to come with me to the police station. A formal statement will be taken from you,' and then you'll be brought home.'

.   .   .   .   .

Downstairs, before they left the house, McCool made sure that he had the Soneryl tablets in his pocket. He asked Mrs. Wimpenny about aspirins, and was shown half a dozen in a bottle. And there was no such thing as a razor blade in the house. He instructed Rannard to be alert for the smell of gas, and that was as much as he could do to prevent a suicide attempt by Mrs. Brotherhood.

On the way to Headquarters Mrs. Wimpenny broke a long silence to ask: 'Is it true you won't open that envelope?'

'Quite true. It won't be opened without Mrs. Brotherhood's knowledge.'

'She didn't write it because she was afraid of Raymond, you know. She wrote it so as she would have a hold over him, and make him keep away from other women.'

McCool's reply was polite but meaningless. He assumed that Ursula had had at least a subconscious fear of being killed, otherwise she would not have felt the need actually to write her statement. He reflected on the irony of the situation. Jo Tavenant had coolly watched her husband's infidelity in order to collect a handsome divorce settlement, and—though McCool could not yet see how—she had lost her life as a result of another woman's frantic and indiscreet efforts to keep a faithless husband in order.

.   .   .   .   .

It was five o'clock when McCool went for Brotherhood. He thundered on his door to rattle his nerves, and loudly demanded admission in the name of the law.

Brotherhood needed no rousing. He was at his bedroom window in a matter of seconds. And he showed that his nerve was still unbroken.

'Is there any need to make all that racket?' he demanded. 'What the devil do you want?'

'I want a few words with you. Come on down and open the door.'

'Oh, go away and come back in the morning.'

'It's morning now.'

'It's still dark. Come back at a reasonable hour.'

'No. My business can't wait.'

The man at the bedroom window moved, as if he were about to close it. 'It'll have to wait,' he said.

'Hold it,' said McCool. He had actually lowered his voice, but it stopped the other man. He continued quite softly: 'I have a search warrant. If this door is not open in one minute, I'll break it down.'

Brotherhood exhaled a sigh of exasperation. 'All right, I'll come down.'

McCool wasted no time when the man opened the door. He said: 'I also have a warrant for your arrest, for the capital murder of Selwyn Sayle, and I caution you that anything you may say will be taken down in writing and may be given in evidence.'

'You're insane.'

McCool nodded, as if that was the reply he had expected.

173

'There's a little more,' he said. 'You will also be charged with the attempted double murder of Ursula Brotherhood and Rowena Wimpenny.'

Evidently Hard Times and Pettit had succeeded in remaining undetected when they had followed Brotherhood home from Witchwood. The charge of attempted murder was obviously a complete surprise to him, and a great shock. His pallor became greenish, and he swayed on his feet, just once, as if he had been gently pushed. But his expression did not change. He stood looking at the policeman with glittering eyes.

McCool turned to Hard Times. 'We'll wheel him in straight away,' he said. 'Go with him and stay with him while he gets dressed, and observe every move he makes.'

A shifting of Brotherhood's feet warned him then. He moved head and shoulders quickly. A blow aimed at his face missed him completely.

Almost absentmindedly he blocked a second wild swing. He seized the man, and held him firmly. 'Stop that foolishness,' he said sharply. 'That'll do you no good at all.'

Brotherhood slavered with hate. 'You swine! You sly, shifty swine!'

'That's a compliment, coming from you,' said McCool dispassionately.

Hard Times had moved in on the other side of Brotherhood. He took over, propelling the man irresistibly towards the stairs. 'Get on, you,' he growled. 'And if you want a Donnybrook where there's nobody looking, I'm your man.'

The two men went upstairs. McCool returned to the door and called in the remainder of his men, who had been waiting near the gate. He briefed them and sent them into the house. Then he went out into the garden and looked up at the sky. There was no prospect of rain, and he was thankful. There could be no effective search out of doors until daylight. So he had an hour or two during which he

174

might talk to Brotherhood before he came back to direct the search. He shook his head. He had not much hope of cracking Brotherhood. It was his opinion that the man would go to the gallows without an admission, without a confession and, at the last, without a word.

     •   .   .   .   .   .

At seven o'clock McCool was in Brotherhood's garden again. As he looked around he reflected that the lady of the house had green fingers.

'Look at that lawn. Not a blade of grass out of place,' he commented. The five detective officers grouped near him nodded in glum agreement. They had found nothing of interest in the house.

'Nothing out here either, I'm betting,' Pettit said.

Hands in pockets, McCool strolled to the dog kennel. He touched it with his foot. 'Turn me that over,' he said.

The kennel was turned over. Obviously the ground beneath it had been undisturbed for a long time. The kennel itself was examined. 'Nothing there, sir,' was the report.

The garage and the shed were searched. The shed was tilted, to show grey, dry, undisturbed earth beneath its floor. The clothes-line posts at each corner of the back lawn were lifted from their sockets, and the sockets explored. There was nothing.

McCool gazed thoughtfully at the overgrown privet hedge of the adjoining garden. 'Beat along that hedge,' he said. 'There might be something.'

As the men moved stooping along the hedge he dwelt upon the mentality of Raymond Brotherhood. The cuckoo mentality. Lay your eggs in someone else's nest. He went and broke through the hedge, at the place where he had penetrated it some hours before. He stood in the neighbour's neglected garden and looked up at the blind windows of the house. Nobody was astir, because it was Saturday morning.

He was reminded of the story of the clergyman, chiding the villager for his pride in his garden. 'You and God, John,' the vicar had said. 'Aye,' John had replied. 'But you should a-seen it when God 'ad it on 'Is own.' On this little plot nobody had interfered with the work of nature for some time. It was waste. And the crumb of earth found in Jo Tavenant's flat had come from waste land.

He walked to the back of the house and looked at a patch of couch grass, docks and dandelions. He turned and went back to the hedge.

'Found anything?' he asked.

'Nothing, sir.'

'All right. Come through here. All six of us will move in line and traverse this little wilderness here. We'll move along slowly, gently pulling at weeds. Gently, I mean. I'm hoping we'll find some which come up more easily than they ought.'

The line was formed and its members moved along slowly, plucking at the weeds. They had almost completed the first traverse when Hard Times called from the furthest corner. 'Here, I think,' he said.

He had lifted up a spread of couch grass in one handful. It had covered an area two feet square. He had needed to break no roots, and there was no root of any other weed visible. 'Somebody rolled this mass of twitch out of the way like the edge of a carpet,' he said. 'He's been digging here. Then he's stamped the ground flat and put the twitch back.'

McCool nodded, thinking of Brotherhood. He imagined the man creeping out to bury his treasure in the half-light of earliest dawn, when police observers would be least vigilant.

Without instruction Hard Times ran to break through the privet. He returned with a small spade, ladies' size. He thrust it deep into the ground on the edge of the uncovered area, then prised up the soil. There was something buried about four inches deep.

'It's hard,' the sergeant said. 'He's put it in a box.'

Soil was cleared away, and a square parcel was revealed. It was wrapped in several layers of transparent plastic. The men lifted it out of the hole, and then they saw what it was.

'A bloody tape recorder!' Hard Times said in disgust.

But McCool was delighted. 'Just the job,' he crowed. 'This is it. Sergeant, you found it. Now you can go and get Superintendent Glenn out of bed.'

18

DAINTILY holding her third martini, Chérie Sayle looked
at McCool with sparkling eyes. They were sitting some
distance apart on a long settee in the lounge at Fairlawn.
With each drink she had closed the distance a little.

'Mr. McCool, it's the darlin' man you are,' she said, in a
creditable imitation of the brogue. 'You've been wonder-
fully clever. How did you come to suspect Raymond so
soon? From the start, almost.'

'Because, at the start, he succeeded in astonishing me. He
told me, before I knew what day it was, that the murderer
had made a mistake. He said that the man should have
emptied the cash box and replaced it in the safe. He could
have re-locked the safe and returned the keys to Mr. Sayle's
pocket.'

'Well, that's reasonable enough.'

'For a civvy who has just walked on to the scene of a
crime, I thought it was reasonably smart. Later, he gave an
explanation as to why the man had made the mistake. He
said he must have felt pushed for time. That was reasonable,
too.'

'Well?'

'For an accomplice of Rodrick to have taken the cash box
wasn't such a big mistake as all that, but for somebody who
wasn't an accomplice, somebody who wanted Rodrick to
carry the can back, it was a hell of a mistake. It cleared
Rodrick. Brotherhood perceived that, all right, and it was

the first comment he made. It was on the surface of his mind, worrying him, no doubt. About the other thing, can you imagine the pressure on a man who has just murdered his boss, and can expect a policeman to arrive any minute? His fingers would be trembling and he would hardly be able to breathe for nerves. He wouldn't be able to think as clearly as he had done when he was contemplating the crime. He was pushed for time, all right. There would be only one thought in his mind—to get out of there with the booty. Again, that experience was on the surface of his mind. It came out too glibly for me. In other words, for a man unversed in police work he made observations which were too acute and accurate, too early.'

'Dear boy, you're too subtle.'

'I'm not saying I was convinced he was the murderer. I merely had a strong suspicion that he was somehow involved, and I had him watched in the hope that he would lead me somewhere. Later I talked to a person who knows him very well, and I was told that he was a man who would think before he moved, and even then he would make mistakes. Some habitual error in the logical sequence of thought, I suppose. That helped to confirm my first impression.'

Mrs. Sayle moved a shade nearer. 'You've been even more clever than I thought.'

McCool shrugged. 'He had us all beaten on the Tavenant job, till we found the tape recorder. *He'd* been even more clever than *we* thought. In the first hour or two of police surveillance he must have realized that he was being watched, and he made his plans accordingly. He had a tape recorder from his own office at Sayle's, one which he'd had for months and seldom used. On the night of the Tavenant job he did a bit of amateur cabinet-making in his workshop upstairs. He made a tape of it, whistling while he worked. Then he set it running and departed unseen. He was gone for an hour. Enough time to get to Regency Terrace and do

179

what he thought he needed to do, and return. While he was away his wife nipped upstairs and undid the bun in her hair. She smoothed it down as well as she could, and put on one of her husband's coats to hold the hair in place and give her shoulders a bit of bulk. She allowed her shadow to be seen in profile on the curtains, and the policeman outside naturally assumed she was Brotherhood. She did that little act a couple of times in the hour.'

'I wouldn't have thought she was so much like Raymond.'

'If you study their faces, you'll see that she is. And, you must remember, a tall woman is about the same height as a medium-sized man.'

'Can you prove it was all done that way?'

'There is some evidence. Three of her hairs were found on one of Brotherhood's coats, on the inside of the collar. And the tape recorder turned up trumps. Through inexperience, or lack of time, or maybe through a mechanical fault, the record of the sawing and hammering was only partially erased. The source of the machine can be proved, and it has Brotherhood's prints on it. He might have taken it back to the office, but I think he overestimated the intelligence of my fellows. He preferred to bury it instead, and perhaps dig it up again when everything had blown over. Then of course there's Mrs. Brotherhood's statement. She was like a child in the hands of an expert like Glenn, and she told what she knew. She's an accessory, you see. But of course she'll retract her statement at the trial.'

'Has Raymond made a statement too?'

'No, and he never will, in spite of Glenn's efforts. He's done us in the eye over the stolen money, too. The thing is, when you bury something bulky, you've got surplus soil when you've filled in again. After finding the tape recorder we found the surplus and we thought there was too much of it, and some of it contained dead leaves. So then we found the money buried in a clump of large and ancient shrubs. But it wasn't on Brotherhood's ground and he won't admit any knowledge of it. I can see now another reason why he had to take the cash box as well as the money. There's ten thousand pounds in ones and fivers, all used notes. That box must have been crammed so tight that the money would have made a parcel twice as big if it had been taken out. And he wouldn't feel he had time to do it. In other words, both his nerve and his brain failed him at the crucial moment. He should have filled his pockets with fivers and left the rest. Or maybe he was too greedy to do that.'

'What will happen to the money?'

'Blessed if I know. I don't see how it can be declared treasure trove, so, if Brotherhood persists in his denials, I suppose it'll become the property of the person on whose land it was found.'

'A nice windfall for him.'

'Yes. I daresay he can do with it. He's got a big family. But that money ought to be yours, you know.'

'No. I wouldn't want that kind of money. If the man with the big family gets it, it'll be an ending which pleases me. He'll be happy and I'll be happy, and there'll be no awkward questions from the tax people.'

'I think Brotherhood exaggerated that danger, to make you want to get rid of the business, with him superintending the sale of it.'

'He wouldn't have done that. I'd like to sell out, or be taken over, but not at the price he had in mind. I wasn't going to let him have anything to do with it.'

'Didn't you trust him?'

'I thought he was honest, but not awfully capable. You see, I've heard Selwyn talk about him.'

'I see.' McCool nodded absently. 'Still, I would like to have pinned that theft on him.'

'Never mind.' There was a little caress in her voice. She reached and patted his hand. 'You've been terribly clever and I'm delighted about the money. And I really am grateful. Suppose he had never been found out, just think what he might have done to me one day. He might have murdered *me* for sacking him.'

'What's that?' McCool's voice was sharp.

'I mean, when he learned I was going to sell the business without his help, and he was going to have a new boss, there's no telling what he might have done.'

McCool was looking at her doubtfully. 'Are you sure that's what you meant?'

'Yes, dear.' She was placating him with the charming insincerity of a little girl trying to escape the consequences of her naughtiness. 'Let us not have any more trouble now. It's all over and I'm very grateful, and I'm going to do something about it. We'll go out somewhere and have dinner, and I shall insist on giving you the money to pay for it. Then perhaps we can come back here and have a drink or two and play a few records.'

'Hot stuff?'

'No! Something soft and dreamy. We might want to—talk.'

'Serenade to a wealthy widow,' he said, to himself. It looked like being a pleasant evening. And towards the end of the evening? Sweet, sweet music, and whatever mood it might develop.

He admitted to himself that he had earned a little relaxation. His work was done. He was moderately certain of a conviction in the Sayle murder, and it was unlikely that Brotherhood's other crimes would come to trial. He did not yet know whether trial would proceed on the capital murder charge, nor did he care. Punishment was not his concern. His business was the clearing of crime and the proper assembling of evidence. In that he had done his best, and done well.

But he was still curious about Mrs. Sayle's slip of the

tongue, if it was a slip. And there was one little thing about which he had had no explanation.

'There's one small item I still haven't a clue about,' he said.

'And what's that?' She was happily interested.

'Last Monday night. You told me you hadn't been out since dinner. You had, you know.'

Her smile became enigmatic. 'How do you know?'

'Your Facel Vega had been out. You told me an untruth, I think. If your going out had the slightest connection with the case, would you care to give me the truth? Then we can close the book.'

She put her glass to her lips and sipped, and looked at him with her head on one side. 'Promise me you won't be cross when I tell you,' she demanded.

'All right. I promise.'

'And you won't start any trouble?'

'Ah, wait a minute. Suppose it's something a policeman can't overlook?'

'You'll have to overlook it.'

He thought about that, and did not like it very much. But if he did not give his word, she would not tell him anything.

'All right,' he said. 'No trouble. Word of honour.'

'Very well,' she began. 'I did go out that night. No, I'll begin at the beginning. Selwyn came home from the shop rather later than usual, and he was in a bad temper. I asked him what was the matter and he said: "Raymond's been blundering." Then he said he'd have to go back to the shop to put everything right, before they opened in the morning.

'We had dinner, and he went back to the shop like I told you. He hadn't been gone more than a minute or two when Mrs. Brotherhood arrived. She was in a state, and wanted to see Selwyn. It's a wonder I didn't tell her he'd gone to the

shop, but I didn't. I wanted to know what it was all about.
I don't trust women all that much.'

'So I asked could I help, and she told me Raymond didn't
know she'd come. She said Selwyn had sacked him just
before closing time, for putting a wrong price on a new line
of goods. I didn't ask what. She said she'd come to ask
Selwyn to give him another chance. Well, I knew Selwyn
didn't like her. He'd had Raymond a long time and he was
worried, and he might have changed his mind about sacking
him. But not if she interfered. She would only have made
him vindictive, and ruined any chance Raymond had. So
I said I had no idea where he'd gone, and I offered her a
drink to calm her down. She said no, she wouldn't stop
because she should have met her sister at nine o'clock, and
it was after that already. So I asked how she'd come out to
Chestnut Park, and she said "On the bus," so I said I'd get
my car out and run her back to town, and that's exactly
what I did.'

'Where had she arranged to meet her sister?'

'I asked her that, when we were in the car. She said:
"Drop me before we come to Commonside. I know where
she'll be." I thought it was an odd thing to say when they'd
arranged to meet, but I put it down to the stress and strain
she was under, and thought no more about it. I stopped
near the end of Commonside, and she got out and went
along that narrow street that runs behind. I watched her
go. I felt very sorry for her.'

McCool put his head in his hands. 'Oh dear, another
of 'em,' he moaned. 'Another unpredictable woman who
could have given me a line and saved me a lot of doubt and
worry, and she says nothing. To me she says nothing.'

She was near enough to put a consoling hand on his
shoulder. She uttered words of contrition, but he suspected
that she was not absolutely serious.

'Brotherhood had been sacked,' he said brokenly, 'but he

was canny enough to guess that his boss wouldn't have bothered to tell you. Only the two of them knew, and of course his wife. Motive, motive, motive. And I wasn't told.'

'Ah, diddums,' she said.

'Why?' he demanded. 'Why didn't you tell me?'

'I thought the poor woman had had trouble enough for one day, I didn't see that it would do any good to tell you about her. So I told a little fib.'

'Well, it doesn't matter now, and that's a fact,' he admitted. 'But don't you see how it could help to establish premeditation? I thought the whole thing was coincidence, and it was nothing of the kind. The only coincidence was Johnny Rodrick's arrest, something which would look like a lovely piece of luck to Brotherhood. He was there lying in wait for Mr. Sayle. The two women were there to spy on him. Even though there had been the calamity of Brotherhood losing his job, his wife was still determined to stop his shinanigans. Because Mr. Sayle took time out to park his car in Herder Street, she was probably in Commonside before he was. Anyway, if she didn't see him go into the shop, Mrs. Wimpenny certainly did. She's the one who'll give evidence.'

'So there you are, it doesn't matter.'

'It might have mattered,' said McCool sternly. 'Never withhold evidence.'

'You know, I never suspected Raymond, but I had a funny feeling when I saw you and him together. You looked at him like—like a lazy tiger. Any minute, I thought, you might reach out and grab him.'

But his thoughts had returned to Mrs. Brotherhood. 'I always wondered how he pressured her to help him fake that alibi,' he said. 'I see now that he wouldn't need to. All she wanted was a home and a husband with a job. When his job seemed to be safe once more, she would willingly help him to get rid of the only menace, Jo Tavenant. Once that

185

was done, everything would be lovely, with herself being able to dangle a rope under his nose to keep him in order.'

'Oh, let's forget it,' said Mrs. Sayle. 'We'll go out to dinner. Excuse me, while I get ready. I won't be a minute.'

She left him. He helped himself to another drink, and sipped it reflectively. It was an unusual occurrence, for him to be taken out to dinner at the conclusion of a job. If he had been a private investigator—you and Philip Marlowe —he might have been more accustomed to such practical expressions of gratitude. What would Marlowe have done in these circumstances? Finding that the lady had added to his worries by not telling him the whole truth, Marlowe probably would have arisen and silently departed, leaving her to wonder whether he was a man or a character of fiction. Yes, Marlowe would have done that.

But Marlowe was not a proper copper. A proper copper did not do himself out of a good dinner. Nor did he disappoint a lady when she was kindhearted, and grateful enough to make a delicate suggestion that her intentions were amorous.

She returned, looking radiant and beautiful in a mink coat. He arose and solemnly took her in his arms, and kissed her. She pressed against him with sudden, candid urgency.

'Oh, oh,' she breathed. 'Must we go out just this minute?'

Ah well, he thought, meals were served as late as eleven o'clock in some places.

>>> If you've enjoyed this book and would like to discover more great vintage crime and thriller titles, as well as the most exciting crime and thriller authors writing today, visit: >>>

The Murder Room
Where Criminal Minds Meet

themurderroom.com

www.ingramcontent.com/pod-product-compliance
Ingram Content Group UK Ltd.
Pitfield, Milton Keynes, MK11 3LW, UK
UKHW040436280225
455666UK00003B/101